THE
INVISIBLE
ENTENTE

A PREQUEL NOVELLA

KRISTA WALSH

To Angela —
I hope you enjoy the new adventure!
Krista 06|18

Raven's Quill Press
Ottawa, Ontario

Raven's Quill Press
www.kristawalshauthor.com

Publisher's Note: This is a work of fiction. Names, characters, places, and incidents are a product of the author's imagination. Locales and public names are sometimes used for atmospheric purposes. Any resemblance to actual people, living or dead, or to businesses, companies, events, institutions, or locales is completely coincidental.

Book Layout ©2013 BookDesignTemplates.com
Cover Design ©2016 Ravven (www.ravven.com)

The Invisible Entente: a prequel novella / Krista Walsh. -- 1st ed.

To Chris Reddie, for helping me get these characters out of my head and into a locked room

From all I've read, the word 'entente' is defined as 'a friendly understanding or informal alliance between states or factions.'

I don't think we're what the dictionary had in mind.

1

THE INTRODUCTION

How would you react if you found yourself trapped in a small, dimly lit room with a group of strangers?

Seven people, three men and four women, found themselves facing this question one previously uneventful Thursday evening. A moment earlier, they had each been engaged in their regular routines — work, homework, watching television — and then the world had changed without warning.

In a bright flash of light, they'd been teleported into a room with no doors or windows, unnaturally bright under the light of a half-dozen candles in wall sconces. The walls were brown stone, the floor just as drab, and the air stank of dampness and disuse.

"—extra fries..." one man said, caught mid-sentence, and then trailed off. He craned his neck to gauge the room — his gaze, hidden behind a pair of reflective, round sunglasses, lingered on the wooden round table in the middle of the room and the seven chairs set around it — and appeared more confused than alarmed by his situation. "Okay?"

He stood around six foot two, tall by most standards, but four inches shorter than the tallest man present. Broad-shouldered and tanned, with an easy smile, a smooth jaw line, and thick brown hair, he was the sort to stand out in a crowd. In the few moments since the group had appeared in the room, he had already drawn the attention of a heart-stopping woman in a curve-hugging green dress. Her brown eyes flashed gold as she widened her lips in a smile that showed off even white teeth. She had popped into the room mid-stride, but adjusted to the change of scenery with the ease of one accustomed to the extraordinary.

"Not the nicest view," she said. Her smile faded as her gaze landed on a man in a gray tailored suit standing across from her. The man shared her honey-hued complexion, her thick gold-touched brown hair, and her delicate construction of fine nose and high cheekbones. Although his presence had lured the eye of another woman with short blond hair, who had tumbled to the floor on her entrance, his powers of attraction apparently had the opposite effect on the woman in the green dress. "Or the greatest company."

"I couldn't say," another woman said, this one hardly more than sixteen years old, her blond curls unruly and tied into two wild pigtails. She wore jeans and a plain black T-shirt with a red-and-white plaid shirt over top. Curved white plastic stretched from behind her ears to transmitters implanted on the sides of her head, and she stared blankly into the shadows through square brown-tinted sunglasses. She'd appeared in the room on her stomach, as though she'd been lying down at her previous location. Cautiously, she crept her fingers along the uneven stone tiles and slowly rose to her feet. Unseeing, she tilted her head toward the sound of a scowling man shifting on his feet beside her, this one wide and hulking, standing at least six foot six with angry red scars down the right side of his face, his hands clenched into fists at his sides.

"I don't suppose anyone could tell me where I am?" the girl asked. "Or who you are? Or how I got here? Pretty sure I was in my room studying for an exam."

"You know as much as I do," said the blond woman who had been attracted to the man in the suit. Her short-cropped hair framed a thin, angular face. Green eyes stared out over a long, bent nose, her thin lips pale. She stood up, crossed her arms over her gray hooded vest, her clenched hands stretching her long-sleeved blue T-shirt, and glared around the room.

The fourth woman remained silently poised on the fringes of the group. She was tall and willowy with waist-length red hair, clothed in a simple, belted blue dress. Although she said nothing, she missed nothing. Her cold gray eyes shifted from person to person, evaluating their reactions, assessing the situation.

The man in the suit loped jauntily toward the wide table. He pulled a hand out of his pocket and reached for an envelope sitting in the center of it.

"Maybe this will give us some idea."

2

....

THE LETTER

Welcome to you all.

While I would normally hate to start things off with a cliché, I can't resist the temptation to say: If you're reading this note, I'm already dead.

I find even more pleasure in the idea that one of you will soon join me.

I don't know which one of you will — if I did, you wouldn't be in this situation — but I enjoy the thought of you all piecing the puzzle together.

Why me? you might be asking. You should really give yourself more credit. I've crossed a number of people in my lifetime, but only you were special enough to make it on the shortlist for my murder. You have been my greatest competitors and my greatest enemies, the only people smart enough or strong enough to best me. As such, I have no doubt you'll be able to work out this mystery.

Since I know you so well, I know you're also wondering why I arranged this little meetup. I'm well aware I've always had a knack for getting people to hate me, but that's never stopped me from working for what I wanted. Right up to the end I was focused on becoming the greatest warlock the world has ever seen — I came close, too, I'd like to see you try to deny it — but just as I was reaching the pinnacle, I ran into an old friend of mine. A Seer. Lovely woman that she was, she told me, right before I cut into her brain, that she'd had a vision of me dying before I achieved my goal.

Having known Cass for ages, I didn't waste time not believing her or going out of my way to try to avoid her prophecy. Instead, I opted to set up this counterattack. I decided that if I were going to die, my killer shouldn't be allowed the luxury of living.

So I created this room and tagged each person I encountered who I believed stood a chance of beating me. At the moment of my death, you were transported here.

Don't bother trying to escape. There are wards on every exit and all of your magical abilities have been blocked. There is only one way out: discover who killed me — and return the favor. Seven enter, six leave.

So work it out, take your time, get to know each other. It should be quite the discussion — I only wish I could be there to see it. The semi-goddess, the Gorgon-Fae, the incubus, the succubus, the daemelus, the sorceress, and the human — such a unique collection for this invisible entente.

Good luck to you. And to the guilty party: see you soon.

Jermaine

"Well, that's just wonderful," said the blond woman. "Of course I have that kind of time."

"Magic?" asked the younger woman. "You're not serious. And what was everything else he said? What's a daemelus?"

"You must be the human," said the man in the suit, staring down his nose at her.

"I'm part machine, baby," she replied with a grin.

"You fixed your ears but not your eyes? Did you forget?" he asked.

"Parents' choice," replied the human, with such finality and speed there could be no doubt she was used to answering the question. "I don't know of any magic technology that makes the blind see, and I don't have any interest in changing who I am."

"That's quite the contradiction," he challenged. "You deny your humanity when accused of it, but cling to it instead of making life easier for yourself if you had the opportunity."

The girl raised a shoulder. "I'm still human enough to be inconsistent, I guess." She turned her back on him and asked the rest of the room, "So, what's a daemelus? Or a semi-goddess? This guy on drugs?"

"You ask a lot of questions, kid," said the man with the sunglasses, his voice warm and lilting with amusement. He reached for the letter the Suit had returned to the table and perused the words. With his mouth twisted downward, he shook his head and stuffed the letter into his coat pocket.

"I've found it gets me more answers than not asking them," the girl replied, and smiled in response.

"That is only true when you direct them to people who know more than you do," replied the sultry woman in the tight green dress. Her smooth European accent slipped through the room like cream, stirring the blood of all who heard it.

"None of you sound too confused about what he's talking about, so I'll assume you're exactly who I should be asking. Can anyone see a way out of here?" The girl stepped forward with her hand out and stopped when she reached a chair. "If not, we might as well sit down."

She scraped the chair back and threw herself into it.

"I don't see any doors or windows," Sunglasses said as he spun in a slow circle, but he didn't appear disturbed by the fact. "That doesn't mean we can't find another way out."

He drew a line in the air with his fingertip. His

amusement faded and his brow furrowed when nothing happened.

"He did warn you," said the man in the suit. His voice carried the same trace of Italy as the tight-dress woman, and the tenor had the same effect on the room, raising the temperature until everyone's cheeks flushed pink.

The blond stared after him as he loped toward the opposite end of the table, two away from the girl, eased down, and crossed one gray-suited leg over the other.

The tight-dressed woman scowled at him. "You needn't be so insufferable." She glanced at Sunglasses and the turn of her lips slid into another slow smile. "I prefer a man who chooses not to take people at their word. Trust is overrated."

She slid into the chair next to where Sunglasses stood and stretched her leg out toward the empty seat beside her. Her expression fell when he went to sit beside the Suit.

The muscular man with the scars lumbered toward the chair between the Suit and the girl and dragged his chair a few inches closer to her, his dark gaze scanning the faces around the table.

The blond woman grabbed the seat between Tight Dress and Sunglasses, and the silent woman, who had continued to stand apart and watch the proceedings, finally eased into the seat between Tight Dress and the girl. Although no words were spoken, everyone around the table unconsciously rearranged themselves to face the silent woman, as though her presence demanded deference.

She stared around the table, and when no one else began the discussion, said, "As we've all been summoned here, we might as well work to achieve the goal our host has set for us."

Her voice came out soft and rich, the sort of voice that might quiet a mob in the middle of a riot.

"Why should I bother?" asked the Suit with a disdainful laugh. "I have no idea how I'm in any way involved."

"He seemed to believe you are," said the soft-spoken woman. Her tone remained calm, empty of argument. She folded her hands on the table, her gray gaze making a tour of the room. "We've been summoned to complete a task that should prove simple with the right logic. I suggest we move forward in a rational manner. To begin, would anyone care to offer a confession?"

The only reply was silence as everyone looked everywhere but at her. The large scarred man kept his eye on the teenage girl, while Sunglasses focused on the wall sconce across the room, and the blond stared at her hands.

The quiet woman pressed her lips into a thin, humorless smile and eased back in her chair. From her, the movement didn't come across as a slouch, as it did with Sunglasses. She remained poised, proper, and in complete control despite the lack of response.

"I didn't think so."

"I don't see why we should cooperate," said Tight Dress, her tone flat. "Where is the benefit to us? He claims one of us is a murderer and wishes to turn the rest of us into the same. Does it not make more sense to find a way out without playing his little game?"

The Suit barked a laugh. "When have you ever had trouble killing anyone? I rather thought you enjoyed it."

Tight Dress squeezed her lips together and refused to reply. The human girl twisted her head between them, her fingers tapping a nervous rhythm on the table.

"You will be safe here," the scarred man assured her.

She cast an uncertain smile in his direction, a clear indication that she had no idea if she could trust him any more than the others.

"I don't really get why I'm here," she said. "I obviously don't run with your crowd, and only met the guy once."

"You must have made quite the impression," Sunglasses said with a smile. "You heard the letter. The only people here are the ones he considered a threat."

The girl grinned. "Then take that under advisement. I may be blind and human, but that doesn't mean you can mess with me."

"You're not the only one who shouldn't be here," the blond interjected. Her nostrils flared and her green eyes were wide as she fidgeted with her sleeves. "Sure, I worked with the guy once upon a time, but I didn't kill him."

The silent woman nodded toward her. "Then how about you begin? Tell us your version of events from the last time you saw Jermaine."

"I shouldn't have to justify —" the woman sputtered, then fell silent under the other woman's steady gaze. Puffing out a breath, she crossed her arms. "Fine. The faster we kick things off, the faster I can get out of here."

3

DAPHNE HEARTSTONE

A three-month hunt for a parajula gem had led me to an empty storefront on the harbor. The place looked shady, but considering how much trouble the damned jewel had been to find, I wasn't about to walk away.

Stirring the air to check for any other presences nearby, I detected someone behind me — but as long as whoever it was minded his own business, I was willing to do the same.

I flexed my fingers by my side and twitched them toward me, drawing a small ball of water from the river. It traveled toward me, settled into the palm of my hand, and I twisted my arm to hide it from direct view. Going into the unknown unprepared would be stupid, and although the small amount of water wouldn't do much damage, I hoped the quality of the river would condemn any potential attacker to a lifetime of unpleasant growths and skin conditions.

I opened the door with my free hand and poked my head into the empty room. Although I had only detected one other person's energy sharing my quiet evening, I called out in case the man I was due to meet had blocked his presence from me.

"Hello? My name is Daphne Heartstone. I'm here to make a purchase."

My mother would have been horrified by my direct approach. She believed we sorceresses should prize secrecy above everything else, but I never saw the point of beating around any bushes. My time was too valuable to waste.

The seller of my gem apparently didn't share my opinion of my self-worth, not yet having shown up. I paced the floor in varying patterns and hummed some Top 40 hit that had been playing when I turned off my car. As the seconds passed and my impatience grew, I turned my attention to the ball of water in my hand. I raised it to the height of my eye and shifted the air currents to create designs with the segmented droplets. A swipe of my hand through the air spread the water into a sheet that stretched down to my waist. In the watery reflection, I saw the shimmer of my narrow face under my short blond hair, my nose ever so slightly too long and crooked, my green eyes a sliver too small. I took in the soft purple sweater over faded blue jeans, which had started to rip at the knees. I raised my chin and set my hands on my hips in an attempt to summon the confidence and power of my ancestors, and then gave a bitter laugh when all the mirror showed me was a scrawny woman who hadn't found a way to live up to her potential.

"Such a shame to let all that raw talent go to waste for some newspaper's benefit."

The suddenness of the voice made me jump, and I cursed as the water splashed to the floor and spattered all over my scuffed leather shoes.

I spun toward the door and curled my fingers so the water ball reformed, the tiny weapon rising to hover over my left shoulder.

"What the hell are you doing here, Jermaine? My deal tonight isn't with you."

He stood in the shadows of the foyer, leaning against the molded archway with a cat-like grin, and I knew he wanted something. He pushed away from the wall and stepped into the moonlit space. The light exposed the rough stubble on his cheeks and the bruises under his dark eyes. His worn jeans and ratty T-shirt added to the impression that he was nothing more than a no-good layabout. I knew better.

He reached into his back pocket, that grin still stretched across his cheeks to show off the clean but uneven teeth within, and retrieved a small pink gem. He held it up to the light to show off the glow at its heart.

With a gasp, I stepped forward to grab it, but he raised it out of my reach.

"Don't be rude. You said you'd come to make a deal."

"How did you get that? My contact for the parajula was Ahmal. Your name never came into it."

Jermaine offered a slow shrug. "When I heard how interested you were in getting your hands on it, I decided I wanted a piece of the action and took over. Ahmal was paid handsomely, don't worry."

From his tone and my sketchy knowledge of Jermaine's business practices, I accepted that my contact was likely dead, which was a pity. I'd worked my ass off building up my network through Ahmal.

I crossed my arms. "What the hell do you want?"

He *tsk*ed. "You're always so angry, Daphne. I'm

not here to cause any trouble. On the contrary. I have an offer for you." He began to walk a circle around me. "We haven't worked together in forever and I thought now might be a good time for a reunion."

I twisted my head to follow him where I could, keeping the rest of my body still and braced for an attack. It had been years since I'd seen Jermaine, and I would have been happy to stretch that time out indefinitely. He was not only powerful, he was tricky. The only thing about him I could rely on was his desire to get ahead.

Aside from our magic, that sense of ambition was the only thing we had in common.

"What do you have in mind?"

He pursed his lips and came back into view on my right side. "A simple spell. Something I discovered in my journey out east."

"What sort of spell?"

With Jermaine, one never knew his flavor of the week.

"One that, by the time we're finished, will let you take that little ball of river water and drown the whole city if you want to."

With a single stride, he closed the gap between us and lowered his voice against my ear.

"You would have the power you were born to

possess, Daphne. Forget your mother and your grandmother — you would step into the power of centuries ago. You would fill yourself with the raw energy of your ancestors. Become a new legend in our day."

I knew he was playing me, but gods help me, every word he uttered set my blood on fire. He'd grabbed hold of my desire, and no matter how much I might want to fight it, I knew I wouldn't.

"Tell me what you need."

He needed a lot from me, as it turned out. Almost his entire plan hinged on having a second magic user on hand, and since I knew I wasn't the only sorceress in his circle, I guessed I was the only sorceress he'd managed to convince.

I decided to ask myself what that said about me at a later time, after the spell had succeeded and I was sitting pretty as the leading crime journalist at the *New Haven Chronicle*.

Jermaine had already done most of the leg work, putting together the checklist and requirements, so it only took another week before we were ready: the full moon overhead, some cemetery dirt in a bowl, and a pig foot ready to throw on the fire. If all went well, I would stand as the most powerful sorceress since the days of Morgan le Fay. The spell wouldn't be the tidiest I'd ever cast, but with all the research I'd done over the last few days, we stood a very good chance of succeeding. Of course, Jermaine would grow in power as well, but as long as the magic was divided equally, I didn't care.

Just a few more hours and everything I wanted in life would be within reach.

My blood hummed in my veins as the ritual drew closer. Jermaine and I were at the empty storefront on the harbor, relying on its isolation to guarantee our privacy.

"I'll go grab the rest of what we need from the truck," he said. "You get started on the circle."

He tossed a box of chalk my way, and I caught it between my palms before it hit the floor. When he stepped outside, I sank to my knees on the dusty floorboards and pulled the spell book toward me to study the design I needed to recreate.

The pattern was simple but detailed, and something about it made me uneasy. I pushed that feeling aside and set the tip of the chalk against the floor, sketching the first lines of the design.

There was no room for doubt — not when success was so close.

I'd just closed the chalk circle when the door

opened and Jermaine returned, towing a luggage cart behind him.

"We all set?"

"We are," I said, but when I saw what he dragged behind him on the cart, that whisper of uncertainty I'd been ignoring rose to a shout. "What are they doing here?"

I stared at the three people stretched out at the bottom of the cart, haphazardly stacked one on top of the other. Their open eyes stared back at me in full awareness, their fear leaving a sour taste in the air, yet they didn't move.

"You can't get ahead without making a few sacrifices," he said.

"We never agreed on human sacrifices." My stomach turned at the idea. All that blood. The cold, terrified glaze in their eyes.

"Don't be so naive, Daphne." He straightened up and turned on me, his face full of impatience at the delay. "You knew this ritual wouldn't be pretty."

"But we never discussed anything about people, Jermaine."

I sensed the rising crackle of electricity in the air from his summoned magic and wished I'd brought some water with me as a defense, no matter that it wouldn't stand long against

Jermaine's power.

He lunged forward and grabbed my upper arm, pulling me close. "You back out now, you die. Understand? I've come too far to have some weakness like compassion get in my way."

Tingles prickled under my skin, a warning of what he would set loose if I didn't comply.

So I let him believe I would go through with it. Dropping my gaze to the floor, I lowered my hands to my sides and tried to appear as though I had submitted to his demands. He only needed to buy it long enough to let go.

And he did.

As soon as his grip loosened, I tore away and stirred the air in the room into a vortex around him, driving up all the dust from the floor in a thick cloud.

Jermaine waved his hands in front of him to clear a space to breathe, his eyes red and watering. I grabbed the opportunity and ran for the door, throwing myself against the cart to roll it outside. One of the dead-weight arms slipped from its place to dangle over the side, the knuckles scraping across the ground. A blast of magic struck my back, and I cried out as I fell to my knees. A tug on my soul pulled me down and made it impossible to stand up. I felt like I was being emptied, as though water were being sucked out of my pores.

"You think I'm as easy to fool as that?" Jermaine demanded, panting. "The spell kicked in as soon as you closed the circle. The effects may not be as strong without the sacrifices, but by the time you walk out that door, your power will be mine."

The hair on my arms rose as his magic surged again, that suctioning sensation driving horror through my heart at the knowledge that it was my magic leaving my body. Fear fueling my limbs, I flipped onto my back and raised my hands in time to block his strike. I folded the air between my fingers and pushed back, hitting him so hard in the chest he lost his balance and staggered backward.

His spell pulled at my veins, and I felt my magic circling. I tried to block it out, but it clawed around the barrier I created.

Closing my eyes, I used what remained of my power to reach out for the water in the harbor. I grabbed it one droplet at a time, my magic rising against his. Behind me, our would-be sacrifices moaned, and I heard the squeak of the cart as whatever drug or spell keeping them down began to wear off.

I tuned it all out and drew the water closer, hoping I had time. While the water approached, I split my thoughts to the other magic tearing me apart. I separated its complicated strands and followed the trail of oiliness to its source in the center of the circle. My hold on the water slipped. I grabbed it again, but forced my attention to stay divided, using my last effort to draw the two spells. My stomach clenched, braced for Jermaine's attack, but I used my power to take hold of the source of his spell and twist it, redirecting its target. The magic formed within me before he noticed what I was doing, and I opened my eyes with a sense of triumph. The ebb of magic reversed, and I felt new strength fill my limbs. Jermaine's strength.

He cried out and released another energy burst, and I rolled to the left to dodge the poorly aimed blow. He looked so pathetic, his bleary eyes still leaking with dust, his nose running.

All I had to do was wait. In a few more minutes, I would have his power, and he would be left an empty shell.

But I couldn't take that chance. He had more power than I, and in the time I needed to absorb it, he could find a way to change the spell's direction again. A half-finished spell was better than me ending up dead.

I glanced over my shoulder to gauge the distance to the door and stepped backward, my hands raised to project a spell of my own. I twitched my fingers and twisted the water into a ball between my palms

Jermaine raised both his hands, tears streaking his cheeks from the dust he hadn't yet blinked away, and the air sparked as the temperature in the room rose. I drew the air around him again as I took another step toward the door, watching the sacrifices out of the corner of my eye to make sure I didn't trip over the slack limbs hanging over the side of the cart. One of the victims had sat up and was tugging at the arm of a woman who hadn't yet regained her ability to move.

A glowing ball formed between Jermaine's palms, and I knew what would come next. Sweat poured down my brow as I fought to keep my own water ball intact, knowing I would have time for only one more strike and wanting to time it perfectly. My heart raced, and my breath struggled with every inhale. Pushing with a last effort, I expelled my magic at the same time Jermaine launched his attack. The lightning shot out from his fingers, aimed between the cart and me, and pain shot through my arm, enough of a burn to take my breath away.

But my water ball knocked him down and the air closed in around him. He curled up on the floor, eyes bloodshot, drenched in water and sweat. From head to toe he trembled, taken over by the chill of having his power drained.

"Looks like you should have taken your own advice, Jermaine. Don't be such a fool. Did you really think I wasn't prepared for you to turn on me?"

"And I walked out," Daphne concluded. "Left the bastard a huddled mess on the floor."

"And the sacrifices?" asked the human girl. Her skin had turned a ghostly white.

"Bolted as soon as they regained the strength in their legs. As far as I know, they all got away."

"This is all well and good," said Sunglasses, "but how do we know you're not making it up? You could have followed him home and stolen the rest of his power until he died."

She ruffled, like a bird fluffing her feathers. "Because I shouldn't have to prove I'm not a liar. If you don't believe what I have to say, what was the point of my telling you at all?"

The quiet woman held up a hand and the argument fell away.

"The only way we'll learn the truth is if everyone shares," she said. "You say you left him alive."

Daphne huffed. "I don't just *say* it. I *did*. Jermaine was an ambitious asshole trying to ride on the coattails of anyone stronger than he was. He wasn't worthy enough to kill, and I definitely wouldn't lie about it if I had."

"But you did absorb some of his power," said

Tight Dress.

"Sure. A well-earned bonus for my unfortunate run-in with that pig. It's not like I gained any new powers — just strengthened what I already had."

The human girl shook her head. "Magical powers. What the hell did I get myself into?"

"How do we know he's the one who started that spell? What if you're draining all of us right now?" Sunglasses's tone suggested he was intentionally antagonizing her, and from the way Daphne crossed her arms and leaned back in her chair with a scowl, his ploy had succeeded.

"All right, then, Mister Idiot Who Wears Sunglasses in a Dimly Lit Room, tell us your story."

Sunglasses's grin widened with Daphne's epithet, and he slouched deeper into his chair. "It'd be my pleasure."

4

GABRIEL MULLIGAN

I sat in the farthest corner of the crowded bar at the smallest table I could find, and still the son of a bitch didn't take the hint.

Jermaine grabbed a chair from the table beside mine, ignoring the nasty look from a man at the bar who had just left the seat to order a drink. He pulled it up across from me, leaned his somewhat beefy frame over the sticky surface, and offered a salesman's smile.

"I believe you took that man's seat," I said.

The words I chose were nothing close to what I wanted to say, but I made it a point to always be polite to the people I loathed. It messed with them in ways that made me giddy.

"I won't be here long enough for it to matter."

"Wonderful. Then how about we skip over everything and get straight to the goodbyes?"

I set my pint on the table and braced my hands on the edge of my seat to push myself off the bench.

"Wait." Jermaine held out a hand to stop me. "Hear me out."

"I really don't think there's anything you could say that would interest me. Or did I not make that clear the last three times you contacted me?"

Jermaine grinned — the arrogant salesman about to make his pitch and believing he couldn't lose.

"Consider my perseverance proof of my belief that you're wrong. I suspect what I have to offer will be of great interest to you."

"Sum it up in two words," I said, hoping to get rid of the peddling quack for good.

And then he had to go and say the only two goddamned words I've ever wanted to hear. The two words that have been my driving purpose for the last thirty-odd years — ever since I became old enough to accept that loneliness is a shitty way to live and there might be something better out there if I could only get rid of my curse.

"A cure."

The smug smile grew wider as my casual pose

froze. For a single moment I lost all ability to hide my longing.

Jermaine slid my glass closer to me. "So why don't you sit back down and we can talk it over?"

I tried to say no. My loathing for Jermaine was nearly strong enough to overwhelm my desire, but the temptation to know — even to hope — surpassed all else, and I sank back onto the bench.

That smile I wanted to punch away remained glued to his face. "Now you're seeing reason."

Jermaine being Jermaine, he took his time coming to the point. He mulled over the beer list, flirted with the blond server in the skirt that only just covered her butt cheeks, and allowed the first three swigs of his beer to linger on his tongue as though it were a five hundred dollar bottle of champagne.

No stranger to his antics, and with no plans to be anywhere else that night — my social life has never been particularly hip or happening, what with my tendency to turn people into stone if I'm not careful — I waited him out, enjoying the knowledge that he wanted to push my buttons and couldn't.

When the pleasure of messing with me wore off

and he realized he'd get no more reaction from me than a blank stare through reflective sunglasses, the shit-eating grin disappeared, and he chugged the rest of his beer down.

"Let's get out of here. Go someplace I don't need to scream anything you'd prefer I kept quiet."

I leaned back in my seat and gestured to the quarter pint still in my glass. "I haven't finished my drink."

In actual fact, the beer tasted like swill and I didn't want to finish it, but I couldn't resist turning the tables on him. And, unlike me, Jermaine hadn't mastered the art of schooling his expression. Each twitch of impatience gave a jolt of pleasure to my cynical, vindictive soul.

A trait I got from both sides of the family.

After the third sip, the sharp bitterness of the stout ran the joke dry, and I rose to my feet, gesturing to the server to add the beer to my tab.

"You come here often enough to run a tab?" Jermaine shouted in my ear as he followed me through the crowd. Because of my tendency to wear sunglasses even inside the dimly lit bar, people chose to step out of my path. Jermaine, being a small man in all possible ways, preferred to follow in my wake. "Why? The beer here is terrible."

"I like it here. People leave me alone." I stared down my nose at him and raised an eyebrow. "Usually."

It had started to rain while we were inside, and I pulled the collar of my brown leather trench coat up around my ears, my chestnut hair long enough now to curl over the tops. Jermaine buried his head under the ratty hood of his sweatshirt and dug his hands deep in his pockets. He tilted his head and squinted into the rain.

"Let's get out of this weather."

I deliberately screwed up my mouth in irritation.

"We were just inside. You wanted to come outside."

Jermaine huffed and turned his back on me, stomping through the puddles down the sidewalk. "Come on."

I smirked at his retreating form. The man was too easy to rile.

He led me to a low-rise building of lofts a few blocks away, the lobby nothing like the shoddy, light-flickering space I'd expected.

"Never took you for living a trendy lifestyle," I said, and peered up into the open ceiling while we waited for the elevator.

"I needed the space. And I've never embraced

the concept of having less than I deserve."

The elevator *ping*ed, and Jermaine slid the cage open, gesturing for me to lead the way.

We rattled up toward the top floor, the glowing red 5 on the button fading in and out.

"I won't tease your patience any longer, Gabe. The truth is the cure isn't finalized yet. Not FDA approved and all that." He flashed a grin, and I squeezed my fists into the folds of my coat, a slow burn of anger tickling the back of my throat. "But it's shown great potential."

"In whom?" I asked, drawling the question. "It's not like there's a wide pool for testing."

"You're not as rare as you think you are, although I'm sure that pretty face of yours makes you think so. We get samples from all kinds of creatures, and we're within a few tests of cracking open the mysteries of the universe. One magic word and we'll have a cure for whatever ails you — scales Bob can't hide, the embarrassing habit Lisa has of turning into a wolf under the full moon — anything you can think of."

I said nothing, but aimed my pretty face at him so he could feel my glare through my sunglasses.

He cleared his throat and shoved his hood off his head. "Look, before you start thinking I brought you here under false pretenses or whatever, I have the studies. You know I'm good for it. I just need some blood. If we add our results to theirs, the cure for your problems could be just around the corner. Within a year."

I let him talk while I focused on taking steady breaths.

The elevator slowed and Jermaine heaved the cage open, stepping out without turning his back to me. Wisely.

"We could make history together, man. You'd have the full use of your eyes." He slapped my arm, and I restrained myself from punching him back. "Imagine that. You already have the face — now you could hit the ladies with a smoldering look without worrying about turning them into art pieces for the building lobby."

His attempt at wit inflamed the restless anger permanently simmering under the surface of my practiced calm, but it also tweaked the heart of my longing. It was true my Fae side had gifted me with nice bone structure and an inability to gain weight on pizza and beer among other things, but my great-grandmother's side, the Gorgon side, had cursed me with a deadly gaze. Growing up had been a challenge, even out in the middle of nowhere where my mother had raised me. More than one child still sat in the park, chipped and covered in lichen.

The idea of losing that curse — of becoming human, even if it meant packing on some pizza weight — filled me with rare hope.

Jermaine opened the door to his loft and flipped on the light switch. Fluorescent light spilled over the open-concept kitchen, the high-shine island gleaming with stainless steel appliances. Two barstools sat at the island and a dining table sat behind me, tucked into the corner.

Beyond the kitchen, in the dim light of the street lights streaking through the rain-spattered domed window, was another large stretch of space. The room was divided between a lounging area, with white couches and a wall-mounted sixty-inch television, and a full laboratory, complete with smoking vials and computer screens with spinning images of what looked like a white blood cell breaking apart.

"Why don't you come have a seat. Can I grab you a beer?" Jermaine gestured to a brown leather dental chair next to the workstation before his head disappeared into the refrigerator's double doors.

"No more for me, thanks," I said. "I had enough at the bar."

The alcohol didn't actually give me much of a

buzz thanks to the same fast metabolism that made me the envy of gym rats everywhere, but I saw no reason for him to know that.

I settled in the chair and picked up traces of fear from the pores in the leather. Years of other people's energy trapped in the fibers.

The effect of the emotions sent tingles through my hands, but while I kept my guard up, the sensation didn't alarm me. I was certain that every dental chair across the mortal world carried the same traces.

"So what's in it for you?" I asked. "I can't believe you're looking to help me out of the goodness of your heart."

I wasn't even sure his chest cavity contained one of those.

The fridge door closed and Jermaine sauntered over, bottle in hand and that same shit-eating grin on his face. "Money. Lots of it."

He set his drink down on the desk and pulled his hoodie over his head to reveal a black muscle shirt with a generic logo on the chest. Never one for classy dressing, Jermaine.

I, at least, wore an open dress shirt over my black T-shirt.

In spite of his soft frame from years of overindulging, defined muscles lurked beneath his flesh. I cast another wary gaze over him, wondering what other secrets he hid behind the unconvincing charm.

He pulled a wheeled stool up beside me and grabbed a vial of clear fluid from the rack to his left.

"This is what they've given me to work with. Not a large quantity, but with the two of us working together, I don't think we'll need more."

Something in his voice — the tremor of...excitement? — put me on edge. "Who's 'they'?"

A hesitation. So subtle I wouldn't have noticed if I weren't listening for it. He'd rehearsed his story well, but he was still lying.

"A company in Norway. They make it their business to study freaks like us." He said it with a wink, trying to bring me into the group. I hated groups. "Of course, a bunch of them are freaks themselves of one sort or another. Some want a cure, some just want to understand what they are."

He grabbed a syringe from another rack and snapped the orange tipped vial to the needle.

"I make it a point to help them where I can. The pay is good and, the way I see it, every step in figuring out what makes us different can only help us put our gifts to better use, am I right?" He held out the readied needle. "Roll up your sleeve for me."

Warily, I peeled off my coat, left it hanging behind me, and rolled my sleeve up past my elbow. In my periphery, I watched him closely, grateful that my sunglasses shielded him from seeing my suspicion.

"A bit of blood and we're on our way," he said, drawing his stool closer.

That trace of excitement in his voice spread to a glimmer in his eyes, and I drew my arm away. "How about you stick yourself with that thing first? Not to say I don't trust you, but one can't be too careful."

Jermaine adopted a feigned pout. "Gabe. After all I've told you, do you think I'd risk everything by hurting you?"

When I still didn't offer my arm, he puffed a breath out between his lips and then grinned. Before I could push him back, he pressed my arm down against the armrest and plunged the needle into my neck. I cried out and grabbed his wrist with my free hand, but the angle didn't allow me to pull him away.

He kicked the stool to the side and threw one leg over me, straddling my waist to pin me to the chair.

"I don't understand creatures like you," he said,

and a second syringe, this one larger and filled with some sort of blue serum, appeared. The needle flashed briefly in the fluorescent light before he drove it between my ribs into my heart and pressed the plunger.

I cried out again, braced my hands against his chest, and forced him off. He crashed into his desk. I rolled out of the chair on the opposite side and yanked the needle out of my neck. There was blood in the orange-tipped vial, so I stuffed the vial into my pocket.

Anyone was free to call me stupid for trusting the son of a bitch enough to come up to his place, but I drew a line when it came to leaving my bodily fluids with people who wanted to hurt me.

My head spun and my breathing quickened as whatever he'd injected into my heart flooded my system. I had to give the asshole credit for being prepared. It took more than an average sedative to take me out, yet his concoction seemed to be doing the trick. And quickly.

My legs gave out and I crashed to my knees, taking the end table beside the couch with me. I couldn't catch my breath, and my vision blurred until I couldn't make out the pattern of the rug beneath me — nothing but a jumble of color that sent shooting pains up into my head.

Jermaine grabbed my arm to roll me onto my back, and I winced at the bright lights overhead. He stepped one leg over my waist and sank slowly to his knees, straddling me once more. As he loomed closer, I saw his distorted features, his eyes bulging and black. My own blurred face reflected back at me across his wide, shining pupils. It took my addled mind a second to realize not eyes but lenses stared down at me. Jermaine's face was obscured by large goggles.

"You have such gifts, Gabriel. Such potential," he continued, as if he'd never been interrupted. I wanted to throw him off again, but my limbs felt too heavy to lift. "If you had more ambition, you'd be unstoppable. No one could stand in your way." He stopped and laughed. "Well, I guess that's not true, but they wouldn't be going anywhere. Your world could be beautifully decorated. But you can't bring yourself to do it, can you?" He slapped my cheek and I barely felt it. "Fortunately, I don't have your reservations. With just a drop of your blood and your beautiful eyes, I can do what you're too afraid to do."

While he spoke, he pulled off my sunglasses. I squeezed my eyes shut and turned my face away, but he slapped me again, and this time the sting sent fire through my veins. I squeezed my hands at my sides and flexed my arms, straining against the weight pulling them down.

"Don't worry about me, Gabe. You won't turn me to stone. Not with these babies on."

I thrashed my head from side to side when I felt the pressure of his fingers around my left eye trying to pull up the lid, his thumb sliding against the socket.

"If you don't want to use these for their true purpose, just give them to me," he crooned.

But he'd put false confidence in his serum. It had kicked in quickly, but had already started to burn off.

With one good swing, I clocked him in the ear, cringing as his fingernails tore into the fine skin under my eye. I grabbed his head and belted him again to knock off his goggles, then bucked my hips to roll him off me.

Getting to my knees, my eyes still squeezed shut, I felt around for my sunglasses. Jermaine's hand slid over my ankle, but I kicked out, my foot connecting with something that crunched under the impact.

He swore and released me, giving me enough time to grab my glasses and coat and escape.

"You gave me a hard time over my story and that's the best you can come up with?" Daphne asked once Gabe wrapped up.

His eyebrows rose over his sunglasses. "Is it your turn to accuse me of lying?"

"It does fall a little flat," said the human girl. "This guy tries to steal your eyeballs and you just walk away?"

"I've got enough on my conscience without adding him to it," he replied, and each word fell heavy on the table with sincerity.

"I call bullshit," said Daphne.

The Suit chuckled. "I believe I must agree with our sorceress. I feel your rage simmering three feet away from me. I find it highly unlikely that in the heat of the moment you chose to run."

"Then answer me this — why would I bother taking the risk of fighting him without my full strength when I could have looked him in the eye and turned him to stone?" When no one jumped in to answer him, Gabe nodded. "Exactly. We might not agree on many things, but I have to side with the sorceress on this one. Jermaine wasn't worth the kill."

Tight Dress's lips had slid into a smooth smile while Gabe told his story, and that smile widened at his last words.

"A man who can show restraint is an irresistible force," she said. "As long as I can be assured that he also knows how to lose control."

The Suit rolled his eyes. "Honestly, Allegra."

"You are in no position to judge me, Antony," she drawled in return, his name flicking off her tongue in practiced syllables.

The human girl cocked an eyebrow. "You two old hook-ups or something?"

Allegra and Antony frowned.

"Siblings," they replied as one, shooting each other dark glances. Then Antony's expression warmed into something slier, and he added, "Most of the time."

Allegra rolled her eyes at the stares her brother's comment evoked, and the murmurs and laughs were silenced only when the quiet woman raised her hand.

"Perhaps it would be more expedient to stay on topic," she said.

"Then how about you go next," said Daphne. "For some reason we all keep looking to you to lead the way, but I prefer to know the woman I'm expected to follow."

The red-haired woman stared at her for three heartbeats, her gray stare direct and considering.

"Very well," she said at last, and crossed one leg over the other.

5

VERA GOODALL

I have spent my entire thirty years trying to keep a balance. As a child, that balance meant finding time to play. As a teenager, it became keeping my friends. Now, as an adult, I focus on running my hole-in-the-wall used bookstore, walking my dogs, and enjoying my solitude. The balance is essential or I face the risk of vengeance taking over my life.

I was seven years old when my consciousness first transported itself into someone else's mind. I'm sure it was just as much of a surprise for the woman as it was for me: the sight of a child-spirit sitting cross-legged in her sitting room. I was too young at the time to understand the complexities, but I knew my mission. It was in my blood.

My mother spent my youth teaching me my role

and explaining my history. She told me how her side of the family hailed from the Norse gods, and it became a sly joke between us that since we didn't have enough gods' blood in our veins for our forebears to consider us the demigoddesses we actually were, we would settle for being semi-goddesses instead. And as the great-descendant of a vengeance god, the burden now fell on me to continue the tradition.

Fortunately, true cries for vengeance don't come nearly as often in our modern era. Most people are happy to lash out in petty squabbles on social media platforms or actively pursue legal justice in a mostly effective system. But every now and then — especially within the circles of people who know of my existence — I receive a summons. A ritual call that transports my mind to a sacred circle where a man can request the death of a lover who had betrayed him or a woman can call for endless pain on a business partner who had robbed her. Then it would fall on me to carry out the deed.

After so many years of practice, I carry no guilt over my nature. I am not a murderer — that title falls on the heads of the people who summon me. I am merely the weapon of choice.

But I became bored of my task. The blood of a god runs through my veins, and the resulting effects make my missions too easy. I have enough strength that a gentle nudge could send a grown man flying into traffic while thinking he'd tripped on a curb. The deaths present no challenge. After twenty-three years, I wished more than ever that I'd been blessed with a sibling who could take over the family business.

So when a bony, hawk-nosed woman named Tiffany asked me to kill a man who had seduced her and promised her the world only to ditch her after their one-night stand, I debated whether or not to accept. Being the end of the business quarter, I had enough paperwork and accounting to fill my evenings, and I wanted to take advantage of the final nice days of autumn to keep up my nightly jog. Unfortunately, used bookstores don't earn the revenue they once did, and practicality won over preference.

"He's scum," Tiffany said, and crossed her arms.

I didn't reply. The reason for her summons meant nothing to me — I needed only the confirmation that she meant it. It wasn't the sort of transaction one could cancel.

"I just want him pushed down the stairs, you know? Something that makes him look stupid and incompetent. Maybe make it look like he tripped on that ugly rug and gored himself on one of his beakers. Can you do that?"

I inclined my head in a nod and watched for any hint of doubt. There was none. I read in her the tragic but all-too-common story of a woman easily led on by the men in her life. Too quick to fall in love, too susceptible to the lies. But she'd reached the end of her patience and this unsuspecting man would be the one to pay for her hurt.

"Bring him to your mind," I said, and peered into her thoughts. It was my least favorite part of the process. People's thoughts — especially angry people's thoughts, which were generally the only thoughts a vengeance worker was wont to see — were jumbled and messy. Loud. Picking through them required effort, even when the person actively thought about what I'd asked them to picture.

It took a moment, but a shape gradually took form in the chaos. A shorter man, not quite stocky, but on the softer side. A man who indulged too much and relied on his metabolism to keep him from becoming overweight — a battle he'd begun to lose. He stood before me in ratty jeans and a nondescript band T-shirt under his gray hoodie. A scruffy beard in need of a trim shadowed his jaw and cheeks. Tiffany thought of him with a warm, charming smile, the sort of man to act awkward and goofy in public, and then be a cozy, teddy-bearish figure at home. Unfortunately for Tiffany, the charm was an act. I'd known Jermaine long enough in my professional life to see past the smile to the sharpness of his brown eyes. His blind ambition and intolerable ego.

Although I usually refrained from forming judgments about either the people who requested my services or the people they requested them against, I found myself thinking that Tiffany couldn't have chosen a more perfect target.

"If you say the word, I'll see to it," I said.

Tiffany's mouth flattened into a straight line as she mustered her resolve.

"I request the death of Jermaine Hershel. So let it be."

With a final nod, I dropped my email address into her mind so she could forward my nominal fee, and vanished.

I opened my eyes to find Vidar, my German shepherd, staring at me. He tilted his head and emitted a low keening noise that told me I'd been gone long enough for him to notice. The stickiness on my face and hands suggested he'd tried for a while to wake me.

I stroked his ears and rolled out of bed, checking the time. Five-thirty in the morning. I was running late. Throwing on my exercise gear, I clipped Vidar and Baxter, my golden retriever, to my waist and hit the streets.

My morning run was my favorite part of the day. No matter what stresses swept around me, this was my time to let them go. I also used the time as an opportunity to plan the completion of my contracts.

Finding Jermaine would be easy. For such a small man, he left a large wake — mostly the stench of putrid immorality, but also of power. How he chose to use his power was infantile, but no one could deny he had it.

My sneakers hit the pavement in a steady rhythm that allowed me to step through my plans. In the early morning no one else shared my quiet loop of streets, so I faded out the houses around me and the sounds of traffic two streets over. I was aware of nothing but the motion of my body and the sound of my footsteps, as paced as a metronome to a melody only I could hear.

Tiffany's idea to knock him into his desk had potential, but left too much room for error. I preferred quick and simple.

The other issue I foresaw was Jermaine himself. Sneaking up on him would be next to impossible — the man's senses were more cat than human. I hated cats. Too unpredictable and untrustworthy.

I returned home and my task faded from my mind as though I'd never had a conversation in the early morning hours through a psychic connection. I showered, fed the dogs, went to work, came home, took the dogs for another walk — all without giving Jermaine a single moment of my attention.

Balance.

The clock struck eight when I took myself to his apartment. The cloudy night blocked the moon except for the slightest glow, and the dying leaves in their breathtaking colors took on the haunted shadows of a coming rainfall.

I pulled the collar up on my white coat to block out the wind and approached Jermaine's low-rise building. The last time I'd been there had been over a year ago, when he'd tried to rope me into some foolish power-grabbing plot. But he had overestimated my interest in power. I possessed what I required to do my job and desired no more.

Choosing a side door instead of the front entrance, I squeezed the handle and pulled until the lock snapped, then let myself into a brightly lit corridor.

I had no fears about being seen — no one ever associated the sight of me with any mishap.

I saw to that.

The elevator took me to the top floor, and I let myself into Jermaine's apartment, leaving the door ajar behind me. He'd detect I was there anyway, but it seemed polite to give him an additional minute's warning.

His apartment was tidy and simple, the furniture sparse and new. None of it looked any more lived-in than the last time I'd been there — except for his home lab. The desk was cluttered with various racks and hot plates, vials, two computer monitors, and some questionable test samples in a glass case. Obviously my turning him down hadn't deterred the man from his mission.

I made myself comfortable and, using the time to my advantage, took a second look around the living room. Aside from the white couches, an ugly red and black carpet stretched out under my feet. Whoever had chosen the décor hadn't done a stellar job at measurement, and the rug stopped just short of the couch. I tucked the toes of my right foot underneath and crossed my left leg over my knee. Then I relaxed into the cushions and stared into the reflection of his obnoxiously large television screen so I could watch the door.

My timing, it turned out, had been near perfect, as he entered his apartment no more than five minutes later. His steps were slow and wary, and I caught his hesitation at the door on finding it already open. The room flared with an abrupt flash of light as he summoned a ball of lightning into his hand, but the magic didn't concern me.

"I know you're in there," he called from the doorway. Stepping inside, he pushed the door closed, the spell still glowing in his outstretched hand. "Show yourself."

I didn't move, feeling no need to put him at ease. He edged farther into the room, paused at seeing my red hair over the back of his couch, and looked up into the television. Although I couldn't see clearly in the reflection, I sensed our gazes meeting, and his shoulders relaxed.

He took three long, slow strides to come around the couch to face me, dropping the spell as he crossed his arms. I folded my hands on my knee and tilted my head to better watch his expression in the dim light.

"Vera. What a not-so-unexpected surprise. I'd ask to what I owe the honor of your visit, but I can take a wild guess. Stephanie?" His brow furrowed when I didn't reply. "Lisa?"

"Tiffany," I said.

"Ah." Jermaine snapped his fingers. "I knew she was a mistake. It's always the clingy ones that have connections to dark magic." He scanned me over. "So what will it be? Broken neck? Poison? Was I already dead the second I walked through my front door?"

The final question came out in a mock film-noir tone, a shifty smile on his lips. Yet under the overconfident expression, I detected a hint of a tremor in his words. For a man so used to being superior in all his encounters, knowing he was at a disadvantage didn't appear to sit well with him.

"I haven't decided," I replied. "Do you have a preference?"

"Um...how about not at all?"

"We both know that's not an option. There was a transaction."

Jermaine released a breath and dropped down on the matching leather chair across from me. He dragged his fingers over his face and leaned forward to prop his elbows on his knees.

"What are my options?"

I said nothing, not wanting to influence his decision.

"All right, what if we both get piss drunk and you push me out the window?"

I shrugged my eyebrows and gestured to the

fridge, an invitation for him to pour.

His eyes darted to the window, and he licked his lips, no doubt thinking about the drop.

"No, if I were going to go that way, I'd want it to be from a height that would leave no chance of some freak survival." His eyes lit up with a sudden idea. "What if we make a deal?"

I watched him closely, and he frowned.

"You're not much of a talker, are you? All right, what if we face off and you try to kill me. You win, then fine, I'm dead and your contract has been filled. You lose, you let me walk. At least you can say you made the attempt. If I ever see Tiffany again, I'll walk with a noticeable limp. What do you say?"

I debated his proposal. While I took my responsibility as vengeance goddess seriously, I also had a great deal of discretion in how I ran my contracts. Not having many competitors in the business allowed me a certain freedom of choice. If Jermaine found a way to best me, why shouldn't he be left to walk away? I guessed it would only be a matter of time before someone else summoned me to try again. And the potential challenge sparked my blood in ways my calling hadn't done in a good many years.

"Very well," I said, and couldn't prevent my lips

from twitching upward when his eyebrows shot toward his hairline.

"Really?"

"I have no quarrel with you, Jermaine. If you can survive me, you can walk."

"Wow," he said, still shocked. "You're decent people, Vera. Thanks."

I didn't want to dampen his gratitude by expressing my lack of faith that he'd win. I was willing to be impressed.

"Let me grab that beer first, yeah? I'm parched. Can I get you anything?"

He pushed off the chair and pointed at me. I shook my head and watched him approach, pass close enough to me that I could have punched him in the side if I'd chosen to. When he was about to step off the hideous rug, I used the foot hooked under the edge to lift it. He tripped, stumbling forward to smash his head against the corner of the granite counter before sprawling on the floor.

I rose to my feet and stepped toward him. He'd left a generous bloodstain on the corner of the countertop, but before I could finish the task, he rolled onto his back with a groan and launched a glowing ball of electricity at my chest.

The force of the attack threw me backward, but the back of the couch stopped my fall. My coat sizzled and smoked, and I tore it off with a curse, tossing it on the floor behind me.

I'd liked that coat.

The magic from the ball skittered across my skin like bugs, leaving behind nothing but bruises.

Bracing my feet against the floor, I threw myself toward him before he had time to launch another attack. With a grin, I grabbed his arm and rolled him onto his stomach, jerking his shoulder hard enough that I felt the pop as it pulled from the socket.

He cried out and flailed against me, but his blows fell numb against my god-imbued strength.

I reached for his neck, and he threw his good elbow back, catching me in the gut. My breath burst from my lungs, and the moment's hesitation gave him the opportunity to flip me over. He leaned forward with his forearm pressing into my throat. Although we both knew I could push him over with minimal effort, I held still.

Blood trickled down his face from the gouge in his scalp and mixed in with his sweat. He panted through clenched teeth, pain etched into every line on his face. I knew I would win in the end, but saw that he would keep fighting until his last breath.

But then he surprised me. With a growl, he shoved me harder against the floor and pushed himself off me. The sudden force smashed my head against the floorboards, my skull leaving a slight indentation as a memento. I rose to my elbows as he reached the kitchen. He wiped the blood from his head with the back of his sleeve and only succeeded in smearing more of the mess across his face.

"I underestimated you," he said. "If you don't win today, you'll just come at me again tomorrow. I know that. Give me one more shot at winning. At least that."

I drew myself to my feet. The challenge of the fight had been fun, but my boredom had caught up with me and I wanted only to be rid of the man. I clenched my hands at my sides and prepared to take a step toward him to finish the fight. It was then I realized my feet were stuck to the floor.

From the kitchen, Jermaine grinned and held up a small metal remote. "Never let your foe reach his tools, Vera. Did no one ever teach you that? Now, I'll do you the favor of not killing you, if you're willing to return it. What do you say?"

I said nothing. My jaw was clenched so tightly with the fury simmering in my bones that no words could come out.

He raised a shoulder in a half shrug. "I'll take that as a yes. But you might want to work on your articulation. Could get you into trouble one of these days. So long, Vera."

Jermaine hit a button and a searing heat cut through me. His apartment disappeared, replaced by an empty street on the other side of town. I collapsed into a crouch, my skin still warm from whatever rune magic had transported me, and I took my time getting back to my feet.

For a moment I thought about returning to his apartment, but the same old boredom that plagued me kept me in place. We'd made a deal. It would be only a matter of time, I knew, and the next time I faced him would be so much more satisfying.

"That was...quite the story," said the human girl. "Characters out of children's stories and classical mythology, now old religions? I think I need to pinch myself to wake up, because this is a whole new level of trippy."

"Please," Antony held up a hand, a wide smile on his face. "You ask us to believe that your entire life's work — excuse me, other than your hole-in-the-wall bookstore, as you so charmingly put it — is to wreak vengeance for those who summon you, and yet you chose to allow this man a pardon? I'm more willing to believe this Tiffany woman summoned you a second time and asked you carry out the contract for which she had already paid you."

Vera stared at him, her gray eyes cold and appraising, refusing to validate his question by answering.

"So tell us curious and doubtful folk," said Gabe, his gaze riveted on the willowy semi-goddess across from him. "You knew Jermaine was a louse and deserved whatever he got, so why did you stop? Why didn't you deliver the final blow when you had a chance or march back up to his apartment and finish him off?"

Vera stared back, lowered her pale lashes in a slow blink. "Because I couldn't care less whether he lived or died."

They stared at each other for almost a full minute before the Gorgon shrugged. "I'm convinced."

"Me, too," said the human girl, raising her hand.

The scarred man glanced at the girl with curiosity.

Daphne grinned. "I wish I could have been there to watch you dislocate his shoulder. That scream would have given me sweet dreams for a year."

Allegra pursed her lips into a pout. "I think it is a shame he is gone. That man's fingers worked a magic of their own."

Gabe raised his eyebrows. "Consider me intrigued. I didn't think this man had any clout with women of your caliber."

Allegra's pout smoothed into a smile that hinted at dark pleasures and sweet temptations. The sort of smile that made a person believe in myths of sirens seducing men to their deaths. "Would you not love to know, Fae. But Jermaine had certain charms."

"Why don't you tell the class, Allegra?" said Antony sardonically. "I would say it's your turn to share."

"So be it, brother mine. Feast your ears on my little tale."

6

ALLEGRA ROSSI

"Allegra, what are you doing? You're up next!"

I'd heard Franco calling me from across the floor for the last three minutes and had pointedly ignored him. Franco was good for nothing except keeping the pace of the fashion show. I had my eye on a much more useful specimen of manhood.

I had spied him almost an hour ago on my first trip down the catwalk and kept a watchful eye on him afterward, too worried that I would lose him in the crowd or that he would get bored and leave.

He was not the most attractive man in the room — I was surrounded by fellow models and B-list celebrities who held much more visual appeal — but something about him made me wish I could step out of the show early to hunt him down.

I licked my lips and headed to the top of the line, taking my place on the catwalk.

The remaining time crawled by, and when the show finally wrapped up, I stepped into the crowd before it dispersed, not even removing my make-up for fear I would miss him.

The mob pushed against me, grabbed my hands, and touched my shoulders. Their buzzing energy ran over my skin like an electric current, and my blood sang in response, craving more. My stomach grumbled, and I distracted myself by redoubling my focus on the faces around me.

On reaching his seat, I frowned. His scruffy bearded face was nowhere to be seen.

And yet...

I closed my eyes and cast my mind around the room, weaving through the energy of every person in it. That power I had sensed during the show remained, and it was close.

"Looking for me?"

He sounded amused to find me, and yet underneath I heard the huskiness of lust. I curled my lips into a smile before turning to him.

"As a matter of fact, I was. You caught my attention while I was up there." I cocked my head toward the stage.

"Was it my eyes or this stunning T-shirt?"

My smile grew. "I was wondering what a man who clearly has no interest in fashion might be doing at a fashion show."

He raised an eyebrow. "How do you know I don't?"

I mimicked his expression, deliberately scanning his basic black T-shirt, old jacket, and ragged jeans, and he laughed. "All right, I was supposed to meet someone. He didn't show."

"That was very foolish of him."

The man frowned, and a spark of anger flashed in his brown eyes. "It really was."

"But I consider it a fortunate turn of events."

His frown faded, and he stuck out his hand. "Jermaine."

"Allegra."

The warmth of his skin increased the current running through me. My heart raced and my breath hitched in my throat. I licked my lips, scanning him over again.

Average height, plainly dressed, and unshaved, with dry skin and dark circles under his eyes...but he had more presence than the highest-titled man in the room.

"I just need to shift into some comfortable attire, but afterward, I would very much like it if you took me to dinner."

His dilating pupils assured me of an affirmative answer, so I left him with a wink and a smile before melting into the crowd and returning to the dressing room.

Lights flickered in and out of the cab as it sped down the quiet, late-night streets.

I sat with one leg crossed over the other and brushed my toe against his calf. Although I noticed his physical reaction to my attentions, he remained a gentleman and kept his hands on his thighs, managing to maintain a dialog without drooling.

"Where would you like to go for dinner?" he asked.

"Someplace quiet," I replied. "Intimate."

Hunger gnawed at my stomach, my head spinning with weakness. It had been too long since I had eaten, and my last meal had been less than adequate.

Jermaine cleared his throat and wriggled in his seat. "If you don't mind beer and leftover Chinese food, I know the most intimate place in New Haven."

I smiled. "That sounds perfect."

He leaned forward to give the driver new

directions, and I rested my hand over his on his thigh. He jerked back — only a momentary reaction — and I heard the hint of a moan in the back of his throat that told me tonight's conquest would be simple.

A few minutes later, the cab pulled up in front of Jermaine's loft, and he jumped to the pavement before it came to a complete stop. He went around to pay the driver and opened my door, offering a hand to help me out.

I accepted, ran my thumb over the center of his palm, and enjoyed the way goosebumps broke out over his skin. I basked in the waves of desire emanating from him.

He led me into the foyer of his building, and as soon as he slid the cage door of the elevator shut behind us, I pressed myself against him and trailed my fingers over his neck, just over the collar of his shirt.

"I hope you don't feel I am being too forward," I purred.

"Not at all," he replied, with only the slightest stammer under the huskiness.

"There is something about you. Something I cannot put my finger on. But it drew me to you from across the room."

I spoke with my lips near his and brushed

against them, tasting his heat.

"I believe the word you're looking for," he caught my bottom lip between his teeth, "is power."

The hesitant, awkward man disappeared, and a stronger one pushed me up against the wall with a kiss so deep my legs trembled. He wound one hand around the base of my neck while the other clutched my hip, drawing me closer, leaving no gaps between us.

I twisted my fingers in his thick brown hair and cast my mind out over his. Every iota of his passion washed over me, ran over my skin and through my blood. I was immersed in the heat of him, drowning and soaring all at once. My body tingled with the energy — so much more intense for having touched him.

The elevator *ping*ed, and he slid the cage open without breaking the kiss. He guided me down the hall, trailing hard kisses down my neck as I grabbed at his T-shirt. We stopped long enough for him to unlock his door and pull me inside, then his hot lips returned to my mouth and his hands fumbled with the zipper on my dress. I kicked the door shut behind me, tugged off his jacket, and yanked his T-shirt over his head, moaning against the warmth of his arms.

I wished I knew what it was about him that made him smell so delicious. He left a craving in me I had not experienced since my first, and I hoped he would be as satisfying as he tasted.

He boosted me up onto his hips and carried me into the bedroom. I appreciated his focus. I didn't want him to pause the proceedings to offer me the aforementioned beer and leftovers. I would feed soon enough.

He toppled us both onto the bed, and his hands were all over me as he shimmied my dress down to my ankles — not the most graceful act, but full of an urgency that drove me closer to the brink. The buzz of his skin set every inch of me on fire, my blood burning with want. Pleasure and desire burst in tiny explosions throughout my body as he pressed against me, his muscles tensed, his shoulders rolling up to his ears as he braced his arms on either side of me. Every time he tried to work his way between my legs, I pushed him back, attempted to get on top — a power play that amused me until my hunger grew tired of the delay.

Grabbing his shoulders, I flipped him over and forced him onto his back, and the surprise on his face told me I had gone too far and given myself away. Unfortunately for him, I was past play time, and he was out of any time at all.

I wriggled my hips and watched the debate in his eyes — the desire to lose himself in the moment versus the knowledge that something was wrong. I loved that part. In another moment or two, as I came closer to my peak, he would start to fight. He would try to buck me off and get away, and the fear would add just a hint of acidity to the taste of him. Enough to offer some zest, but not ruin the dish. Some of my kind hated it, preferred to take their meals at the height of pleasure, but that was too sweet for me. I needed some fight.

The sound of his heartbeat thrummed in my ears, and the salt of his sweat rolled over my tongue as I ran it over his chest.

The pressure inside me grew, my own heart racing as I built toward climax, and I raised myself up to stare down at him, gripping his wrists to keep him still. His face sharpened in my vision, each pore clear and defined as my eyes changed. By the awareness filling his expression, Jermaine had noticed.

But there was more than fear in those brown eyes. There was recognition.

As I raised my guard, bracing myself, my skin prickled with a surge of magic that burned my hands where I touched him. I jerked away, and he raised his hands to send a ball of electricity shooting toward me. I dodged out of the way in time, grabbing the sheet to shield myself. The cotton caught fire, and I dropped the sheet on him, throwing myself off the bed as he flailed to quench the flames.

The instinct to fight for his life was strong, but he had underestimated me. More than anything, I required my secrecy. I had to feed, and if he spread word of what I was, I would starve. I wanted to survive as much as he did. Launching myself at him, I grabbed his face and dug my thumbs into his eyes, squeezing as he tried to pull free. Another blast of energy, this one weaker but still forceful, caught me in the chest, and I flew against the wall, the back of my head cracking against the plaster. I dropped to the floor to avoid another attack, and the wall blew out behind me.

I leapt at him again, but he moved faster and grasped my hair, and the tug of my roots shot pain into my skull. He yanked me back onto the bed and kept his grip tight. Something cold and sharp moved against my throat, and for the moment, I thought it best to remain still.

"Warlock," I spat. "I should have recognized that particular stench you carried."

"And I should have known you were nothing

but a goddamn succubus."

"Why? Because no other woman has ever been so eager to get into your bed?"

The pressure on my hair tightened, and I grunted with pain.

"I should kill you," he said, and I heard a soft inhale as he breathed in the scent of me.

"I would very much like to see you try."

"Either way, you're missing out on this meal."

"Something I have already accepted. Although it is a shame. A man like you would have kept me fed for months. Such power. Such virility."

I stroked the inside of his thigh and felt him twitch beneath me. His grip on my hair loosened and he ran his fingers through the strands, arching his back so he pressed against me.

Then he froze, which made me smile. To feel men struggle against their desire always entertained me.

"So what do you propose?" I asked. "You know my secret, but I do not know you. I have no reason to trust you. Without trust, my options are limited."

Jermaine chuckled. "I know the secrets of every supernatural in this city. I make it a point to know. The only reason I didn't pick up on you right away is because you're from out of town. That right?"

I smiled. "I am from nowhere. Settling down is not good practice for women like me."

"No, I guess not. My point is I keep secrets. No use spreading them around when keeping them assures me allies when I need them."

I narrowed my eyes. "You mean blackmail."

"I don't like to think of it that way. It's not like they don't have anything on me. That balance is how this city functions."

"So you suggest I walk away? That I put my trust in you, try to forget the temptation of the taste of you, and believe everything will work out all right?"

"I want to keep my soul, you want to keep your secret. Sounds like an even trade to me. But I'll tell you what — the day I let your secret slip is the day you can come back and polish me off." I felt him smile against my cheek at the double entendre. "Do we have a deal?"

I weighed my choices. Yes, he knew what I was, but he was by no means an innocent flower himself.

A trickle of relief, starting at the base of my skull, flowed down around my heart, through my belly, and between my legs. I smiled, thinking that as much as I needed to feed, I could think of a few other ways to pass my time.

Sliding my hand up between us, hearing Jermaine's breath hitch, I said, "Perhaps I could be persuaded to let you go, but my demands would be very high."

He chuckled and ran his fingers over my stomach toward my neck and cupped his hand around my throat.

"I don't normally negotiate with people who have tried to kill me, but with you, I might be willing to make an exception."

With a moan, I grabbed his hair and pulled him down for a kiss.

Silence met the end of Allegra's story. An aching warmth hung in the air.

The human girl spoke first, her face void of expression. "That was... graphic. Seriously. I don't think I was legally old enough to hear that story."

"Not to mention — just like all the other stories spouted around this table — it sounds like a bunch of malarky," said Daphne. She adopted a falsetto and exaggerated accent. "'I didn't kill him, I just gave him the little death.' Bullshit."

"Such poetry!" said Antony, his smirk wide.

"Tell me I'm wrong," Daphne shot back. "I knew the guy, and nothing would have induced me to sleep with him."

Allegra grinned. "And unfortunately, now you will never get the chance. He was so good, I would not have minded a second go."

Gabe chuckled. "It'd be easy to believe you're trying to distract us from the real story by pandering to our more primal sensibilities."

She flashed her smile in his direction. "I confess part of my goal was to put images in your mind of what I am capable of doing."

"You were always one of the more skilled in the

family," Antony said flatly, and Allegra laughed.

"Credit where credit is due, brother. Your skills always rivaled mine."

The human girl released a soft groan. "Another soul-eating sex monster?"

Vera extended her hand. "Would you care to go next?"

Antony's bright smile, as sly and alluring as his sister's, grew, and he shifted his weight to switch the leg he draped over his knee.

"I'm sorry to disappoint everyone, but I have the most mundane tale out of all of us. Mine doesn't even involve a fight."

"Indulge us, brother," Allegra drawled.

.

7

ANTONY ROSSI

We met at a bar. It was Sunday night and between sports seasons, so only the regular drunks were around, slumped over the bar in various stages of inebriation, a few of them sobbing over past woes or railing against the causes of all their troubles. The same pathetic specimens one finds at all similar establishments.

I wasn't there to join them. Alcohol rarely held any appeal for me, and the stench of the fleshy barstool extensions was nearly enough to drive me back into the rain, but I needed the escape. Work had been long and loud; my apartment felt no less loud for its silence. At least the bar had energy, a quiet hum that buzzed through my veins and made me feel alive. And hungry.

When he walked in, he looked just as out of place among the refuse as I did. Yet he greeted the bartender by name and sank onto the far stool with familiar ease. Jim, as the bartender's name seemed to be, brought him a pint without an order, and the man accepted it with a nod before turning his attention to the glare of his smartphone.

I watched him over the rim of my glass, appreciating his rough hands and the muscles in his forearms, which flexed when he pushed the sleeves of his blue hoodie up to his elbows. His chin was stubbled, but the strict lines around the jawline suggested an attentive maintenance.

What struck me most was the raw power emanating from him. So shabbily dressed, he was no doubt easily missed by the masses, but for me he shone as a beacon in the smog of the other men.

Whether it was coincidence he turned around or he sensed me staring at him, I'll never know, but as soon as our eyes met, I knew I'd have him. Having already fed that day, it wasn't hunger that induced me to smile at him, just pure unadulterated desire. The way he smiled back made my body flood with heat.

Not unexpectedly after the silent exchange, he took his drink and abandoned the swill at the bar, sliding between chairs to join me at my table.

"At the risk of falling on tired clichés," he began, and his voice reminded me of rich, dark coffee, "will you allow me to point out that I don't think I've ever seen you here before?"

I increased the charm of my smile, a skill I've always been particularly proud of for what it has helped me achieve.

"You may. The answer is simple. This is my first time here."

"Then that explains that. Mind if I join you?"

I stretched out my hand, gesturing for him to take a seat. In spite of his poor fashion choices, he lifted the chair away from the table instead of dragging the legs across the floor as I might have expected the other cretins to do.

He introduced himself as Jermaine, and when I told him my name was Antony, he repeated it with such perfect inflection that heat shot down from my stomach. In that moment, I didn't think anyone had ever pronounced it half as well.

"So what brings a classy guy like you to a shithole like this?" he asked, raising his beer to the gentlemen at the bar.

"The shittiest of shitty days called for some drinking in a shitty bar, as it happens," I replied, never letting my smile waver.

"And why such a shitty day, Antony?"

And again, the way he said my name made the rest of my day irrelevant. Never mind that the woman I'd devoured that morning had been less appetizing than I thought she'd be, or that my co-worker had once again decided it was wise to steal credit for one of my projects. That the two were related may have explained the reason for both, but none of it mattered anymore.

"I can't remember."

Jermaine's smile widened. "Well, is there anything I can do to make your day better...Antony?"

It was the deliberate tacking on of my name that decided me to invite him home. He'd read me well in the few minutes we'd spoken, and I wanted to discover how well his insight translated to other areas.

He accepted my offer without hesitation and we left our drinks unfinished on the table, the mediocre beer having lost its appeal.

My condo being only a few blocks away, we opted to brave the rain and walk, the cold not touching the heat of the moment.

A few stares came our way as we stepped into the lobby, but the opinions of humans had never meant less to me. His fingers were warm on the back of my neck, his fiery tongue scorching mine.

He tasted delicious, like honey whiskey.

We made it upstairs, the automatic lights spilling a soft golden glow over my mahogany coffee table and burgundy couches. I didn't bother to give him the tour, taking him straight through to the bedroom.

My blood sizzled with his power, and everywhere he touched me created sensations I'd never experienced before.

By nature I'm not a romantic person in any sense of the word, but I knew that something about this stranger could feed me for ages if I ever decided to go all the way. I found myself thankful I'd stepped into that awful dive bar.

For that night, I chose to indulge other desires, but I was determined that, from that moment onward, his soul was mine.

Antony cleared his throat and gave the room a tight-lipped smile. "Sadly, I never had the opportunity to fulfill that other desire. Someone in this room stole that moment from me." His brow furrowed with what appeared to be genuine regret. Then he smoothed out his expression and replaced it with his smile. "But you see? Like I said, not even a fight. Doesn't compare with any of your stories in the slightest. If the rest of our evening got a little rough, I guarantee you, all was consensual and mutually enjoyable. To a very large degree." He chuckled. "Although I never appreciated how similar your tastes and mine run, sweet sister."

Gabe's features expressed a deep incredulity. "I don't know much about your kind, but don't you feed off the souls of the opposite sex?"

Antony's charming smile returned. "That's dinner, dear Gabriel. Jermaine was dessert." The smile dimmed. "But I hope my tale rules me out as a suspect. I've never even been inside his apartment."

"Then why would he tag you?" Daphne asked.

"Perhaps because even the best sex can kill you," he replied, and the silence that greeted his conclusion caused his smile to broaden.

The human girl grimaced. "If you get your soul devoured, I guess. Or unless Gabe turns you to stone first." She shook her head. "How did I wind up here with you people?"

"That's a damned good question," said Daphne. She narrowed her green eyes and crossed her arms with a huff.

Vera silenced her with a look, then said to the girl, "Perhaps you'd care to share how you did come to be here?"

The girl opened her mouth to speak, but before she could utter a word, the large, scarred man beside her snarled.

"She's involved because of me."

"What?" the girl replied, the deadpanned tone giving away her confusion.

"How?" Vera asked.

Everyone else's attention shifted to the man beside her. He squirmed in his chair and dropped his gaze to his folded hands as he began to talk.

8

ZACHARIEL

I had spent months seeking out Jermaine. From all the information I had gathered about him, I should have avoided him as one did a pile of dog shit, lest I carry the stench of his oiliness around with me afterward.

But I'd also learned he was the only person who could help me.

Once I discovered he was in the city of New Haven, I didn't have much trouble tracking him down; fifteen minutes at a computer in the public library had given me his phone number and home address. I approached his place near dusk, when I thought my chances of catching him on his way home might be higher. I didn't enjoy being out during the day. Between the twisted scars on the right side of my face and my six-six, two-hundred-and-fifty-pound stature, my appearance tended to draw attention and alarm.

I lurked in the shadows across from his building, out of sight of most passers-by, and waited a good two hours. The church bells marked eight o'clock mass as he finally appeared.

He got out of a cab — alone, I was pleased to see — and went inside. I slipped out of my alley and made it to the elevator just as the cage door closed.

"You're Jermaine?" I asked, although I knew the answer.

His finger hovered over the button for his floor, but he didn't press it, eying me warily. His reaction didn't surprise me. I knew I was quite a sight to behold, and tried to see myself how he must see me. I loomed over him by a good six inches, and although he wasn't a scrawny man by any definition, my broad frame stretched the corners of my trench coat to nearly twice his width. The red scars on my face tugged down the corner of my right eye, which only chance had kept me from losing. Along with the way my hands dangled by my sides, I imagined I looked very much like some hulking ogre.

In spite of my sinister appearance, Jermaine

showed more curiosity than fear.

"Who wants to know?"

"Someone looking to have a job done that requires your particular...skills."

Another moment's hesitation, then a spark of interest as he assessed me. I forced myself not to look away or bow my head to avoid his gaze. After he finished scanning me over, he slid the cage door open and jerked his head.

"Come on upstairs and tell Doctor Jermaine your troubles."

I said nothing as we traveled to the top floor and trailed behind him after he stepped out. The hallway was brighter than I expected it to be, and cleaner than anywhere I expected Jermaine to live. While the old carpet smelled of cigarette smoke and stale cooking, the walls had been painted within the last year by my guess, suggesting some consistent maintenance. The only exit other than the elevator behind me were the stairs at the end of the hall. I made sure to keep out of his reach and watched for any sudden moves while he unlocked the door to his apartment.

Meeting somewhere outside would have made me more comfortable, but I didn't want anyone overhearing our conversation.

Not that they would believe anything they

heard.

I stepped inside and stayed near the door with my arms crossed while he passed the open kitchen to the fridge. Across from me, the open-concept living room was divided into the living area to the left and a cluttered laboratory-like station to the right, with what I assumed was the bedroom door behind the lab. The easiest escape route was the door behind me, but another door — glass, fitted into the large, domed window beyond the dining table to my left — led to a fire escape.

"You can stay by the door if you want," Jermaine said, "but I'm going to make myself comfortable on the couch. You're welcome to join me." He stepped away from the fridge with a beer in his hand, and I noticed he didn't offer one to me.

He crossed over the rug and dropped down on the white leather couch. He reached for the television remote on the end table and tapped his finger on the power button, but didn't turn it on. In the empty reflection of the screen, I watched him take a swig of beer, which he followed with an audible sigh of satisfaction.

I followed the wall closest to the window and remained standing in pained silence until Jermaine glanced at me over the lip of his bottle. I realized how absurd I looked. With an awkward shuffle, my large frame not made for small movements, I dropped onto the far end of the couch, the cushions sinking deeper under my weight than I had anticipated. I tried to shift myself out of the groove, but each redistribution of my weight only lowered me farther, so I froze.

"Good, that's better," said Jermaine. "I never enjoy looking up at a man when I talk, and with you I imagine I'd get a crick in my neck. So tell me your story. Let's start easy. What's your name?"

"Zachariel."

"All right, Zach, so what do you need, and what are you willing to offer me in return?"

Some people might have been put off by his bluntness, but I appreciated it. I always preferred knowing where I stood.

When I remained silent, wanting to collect my thoughts before I began, he said, "You remind me of a cat, you know that? Big as you are, you're jumpy. But you came to me, so if we could move things along, I do have things I need to do."

I forgot about my precarious cushion balance and shifted again, my hand slipping between the cushion and the armrest before I tensed and slowly righted myself.

"Why don't I kick things off," Jermaine said. He set his beer down on the table and clapped his hands, rubbing them together before tilting his fingers toward me. "You're a demon."

"Half," I corrected.

"Okay, we're getting somewhere. What's the other half?"

I mumbled the answer under my breath, and when Jermaine stared at me with impatience, I repeated more strongly, "Angel."

His eyebrows shot up with interest. He grabbed his beer from the end table and settled back into the couch, his gaze never leaving my face. "Tell me more."

I skipped over most of the tale, reluctant to dive into the sordid family history of my demon mother, with her hot temper and overwhelming bloodlust, and my angel father, his cold purity so sharp it cut through the world like a fine blade. My mother had been the one to tell me their story, how in spite of their differences they'd shared a passion hotter than the fires of either family. The white hot inferno had lasted until my father fell. Cast out of the heavens with no recourse, he had chosen to live homeless on the streets of a heartless city in an alcoholic haze, while my mother had raised me and tried to make the most of living on Earth.

Avoiding as many personal details as possible, I

stuck with the basic facts of my divided bloodlines, and concluded with, "I hear you can help me pick a side."

Jermaine's lips twitched in a smirk. "Tired of batting for both teams, are you?"

I stared at him vacantly, happy to let him believe I didn't understand his meaning. I hadn't come for jokes or small talk.

The smirk disappeared from his face, replaced by a confused frown. "Why, man? You have the best of both worlds right now. Why would you want to choose?"

I swallowed the anger burning the back of my throat and squeezed a fist against my thigh. "Because it's not the best of both worlds. It's having no world. I'm denied by my father's side and attacked by my mother's."

A decade ago, I'd sought out the angels, and when they cast me out for my impurities, I'd gone the other way to unite with my mother's family. The scars on the right side of my face still prickled with the memory of my encounter with the Korvack demons. The demons had mocked me as they burned me alive and tried to tear me apart. Then they, too, had cast me out — a cruel joke to leave me beaten and scarred in a world that would have its own difficulties accepting me.

"I see. So you're feeling sorry for yourself."

"I am not," I growled, and my anger slipped. "I'm just looking for a place to go. Where I can be at peace."

"Why not take advantage of what you have and what you can do? Man like you, I'm sure you could create your own peace."

"That's not the life I choose to live."

Jermaine eyed me over his beer. "Very interesting. So which do you choose? The way of fire and rage, or ice and hard purity? Both sides turned their backs on you — who do you want to crawl back to and beg for more?"

I dug my nails into my palm to hold myself back from punching him in the throat. In spite of his arrogance and rudeness, I had to remember he was my best chance.

"I wish to rid myself of the demon. If I must survive in the world in the guise of a human, I would prefer not to be overwhelmed by my desire to destroy it. This anger is constant and restraining it is exhausting."

"And you think the angel side would be better? From my experience, those warriors are not all fluffy kittens, either."

I glowered at him. "Their justice for impurity is swift, but their anger is cold and detached. I might not think better of the humans who surround me, but I'll be better suited to living a solitary existence, which is what I want. Will you help me?"

"Sure," he replied without hesitation.

His certainty took me aback, and I needed a moment to form my reply.

"Thank you. I am able to pay you."

I shifted to reach my wallet, losing balance again on the couch cushion, but he held up a hand to stop me.

"You can pay me, but I don't want money."

Warily, I asked, "Then what is it you want?"

He grinned and swung himself to his feet. Heading over to his desk, he set down his beer, struck a few keys on the keyboard, and crossed his arms.

"Your demon."

"What?" I scrunched my brow, felt the tightness of my scars as the skin moved.

"In case you don't know, I'm a warlock. It's why I'm able to help you. You're looking to better yourself, and so am I. I'm on a constant search for improvement. And you've got power, my friend. A real, raw strength. On both sides. You're looking to get rid of half of it to improve your life, and I could improve mine by taking it on. What do you say?"

I had known the man for all of half an hour and

didn't like him. I didn't trust what he would do with the extra power — he was too ambitious for his own good. But at the same time, I couldn't afford to care. I had my own ambitions, and I needed to take that one step toward normalcy before I could turn my back on the poorly named New Haven forever. What did it matter what this man did with his city after I left?

"I agree."

Jermaine's grin widened, and he extended a hand toward the long, reclined leather chair. "Then step right up."

I eyed the distance from the fire escape to the chair. I didn't like the thought of being so far from my exit route. But if Jermaine remained between the chair and his desk, I could get out if I needed to.

With a deep breath, I rose from the couch and followed him toward his make-shift laboratory. I settled in the chair and gripped the armrests, making Jermaine laugh.

"Just relax," he said. "This won't hurt a bit."

Such words rarely instilled confidence in the person who heard them, but at first, he was right. As he began to chant over my head, reading the text off his computer screen, I felt merely lightheaded, my limbs attached to my body only in a purely physical sense. My nose tingled, and a sharp burn ran down my throat. Then I moved from lightheaded to numb. With a passing thought, I noted that if this were the extent of the process, I would be just fine.

But the longer the spell went on, the sharper the pain in my throat became. Jermaine's monotonous cadence melted into a hum deep in my ears that traveled into my head until I vibrated with it. Stabs of agony burst behind my knuckles, something sharp tearing at me from the inside. My skin began to itch and, through the haze of pain and dizziness, I watched my arms turn red, like embers against a charred log, the pores replaced by scales.

"No," I said, and the word came out raspy, as if my entire mouth were also covered in rough shell-like scales. "Stop!"

The chant only intensified, but in my mind, I heard Jermaine's voice as clearly as if he spoke in my ear.

"It was your choice to waste your power, Zachariel. I'm just trying to put it to good use. You agreed to let me have your demon. Trouble is, the demon is attached to you. So relax, sit tight, and in another few minutes, you won't remember anything except that you are my loyal slave."

He laughed, and I struggled to break free, but my arms and legs felt too heavy to move, bound by the weight of the spell. Another loud hum overtook the din of the chant, and it wasn't until my mouth went dry that I realized it was my screams. My lungs ached with the exertion, and my mind slipped farther away, nothing but anger remaining. Anger and a desire to bend my knee to Jermaine's will. The harder I fought against it, the sharper the pain in my head became.

Despite my fears of what Jermaine would do with me, I thought about how easy it would be to give in, to slip away and never again worry about having nowhere to go. I'd made a deal with the devil, and I had lost.

The sound of shattering glass yanked me out of my defeatist thoughts, and Jermaine stumbled in his spell, interrupting the flow of magic between us. Then a terrible crashing noise echoed in my right ear, and a puff of smoke rose in a cloud above the computer, accompanied by waves of shooting sparks.

Jermaine cursed and jumped away from his desk, then reached for his papers. He jerked back when the sparks got too close to his fingers.

The shaft of an arrow protruded from the remains of the computer screen.

I looked toward the domed window to find the large pane had shattered. Another arrow lay in the broken glass scattered across the floor and rug.

Taking advantage of the distraction, I swung my fist — still swollen, red, and scaled from the spell — toward Jermaine's head. The force of the blow sent him crashing to the ground in a daze, and the momentum of my swing pulled me out of my seat. I rose to my feet on shaking legs and bolted to the fire escape. On my way out the window, I stooped and grabbed the arrow from the glass, not wanting to be unarmed while I was so vulnerable.

As I fled down the stairs my skin tingled with the effects of the spell wearing off. The strength in my legs evaporated halfway down and I took the last of the steep steps in a roll, landing in a heap at the bottom.

Head spinning and mouth still dry, I crawled to the shadows across the alley. I wanted to find a safe place to recover, but as I turned around, I saw a small figure with wild blond hair and a bow over her shoulder sprint across the street from a tall condo building to Jermaine's loft.

My heartbeat slowed, and although drums were beating an unpleasant, unsteady rhythm behind my left eye, my thoughts settled as my mind returned, the desire to go to Jermaine and ensure his safety fading away.

Jermaine's figure appeared in the middle of his broken window, and I pressed myself against the wall to avoid his notice. I wouldn't put it past him to track me down, but couldn't bring myself to leave yet, too curious about the figure with the bow.

Then I saw Jermaine twist his head toward the door

.

"I can tell you nothing about what came next," Zachariel said, and sneaked a glance at the girl beside him. His fingers tapped on the back of his hand and the knuckles strained when everyone else at the table shifted their attention to the human in silent anticipation.

As though she sensed their gazes on her, the girl nodded, and a deep crevice appeared between her eyebrows. "I suppose this is where I take over, then. Yippee."

9

MOLLY HARRIS

I never set out to be any kind of vigilante, so what happened that evening came as much of a surprise to me as I imagine it did to everyone else involved.

Then again, I'm used to people underestimating me. Fifteen years old, blind, severely hard of hearing, I sometimes impress people by being able to make myself dinner.

My entire life has been an adventure, especially back when I was learning to communicate and become independent. Not that all kids don't face challenges — I just had the privilege of being extra fun for my parents.

They coped well, in my opinion. Making the decision for cochlear implants before I was old enough to decide for myself had opened up one avenue of communication. Growing up, I trained myself to focus on sounds, to pick up cues my eyes couldn't catch. As a kid, I called it my super power. After a while, I outgrew the idea and accepted it was a self-taught skill. Now? I'm not so sure.

At ten years old I developed an interest in archery, and my parents, being the amazing people they are, offered all the support I needed to get started. The sharp whistle of wind around the arrow shaft became my favorite song, and the softness of fletching under my fingers was better than any teddy bear. Between my parents, my coach, and the help of a tactile sighting device, I reached the level of national champion for my age group when I was fourteen.

Last year I agreed to upgrade to the latest model of implant, giving me access to frequencies that were previously cut off. With the change, I felt like I could hear everything, from distances much farther than I would have expected. The sounds added new dimensions to my life, and everything I'd learned and trained myself to pay attention to came more easily, increasing my skills at the archery range.

Nothing compared to the feeling of a bow in my hand, my fingers sliding over the arrow shaft until it fit snugly. With the sighting at my elbow, I could judge my position, and I used the sounds around me to tell me everything else I needed to know. My accuracy earned me something of a reputation in my circles, but I never let it go to my head — or I tried not to, anyway. I spent four to six hours a day practicing, and it felt good to know that the hard work paid off.

Usually.

The day my life changed, I'd come in second in an important competition. I had tuned out the hum of the crowd as usual, but then flocks of migrating birds had passed through the area. The wind also picked up something fierce, and between the overwhelming noise and constant need to correct against the air currents, I kept losing my place. Damn birds were lucky I didn't take them down one by one.

It had taken me a few rounds to wade my way through the distractions, but in the end I was firmly in second place.

All I wanted after the competition was an ice cream sundae with extra chocolate sauce, so of course it was a night my parents had made a commitment to host dinner for their friends. We headed home straight from the range, and I confess I sulked the entire way, feeling in no mood to be social.

As soon as we finished dinner, while the adults relaxed over coffee, I slung my bow and tripod cases over my shoulder.

"Where are you going with those?" Mom asked.

I tapped my cane against the floor, and jerked my head in the direction of the balcony door. "Just to get some fresh air. Maybe hold my bow over the balcony and threaten its life to make sure it behaves better next time."

The semi-joke earned some soft laughter, and I heard my father sigh.

"Try to remember it's against the law to shoot arrows into the sky, Mol," he said, and I offered a brisk salute before escaping to the balcony to take a minute for myself.

I hated feeling off-balance and knew the only way to make myself feel better, if I couldn't get my hands on any ice cream, was to practice. After the day's performance, I told myself I needed the extra time.

The wind was cool and sharp on my cheeks, a fall wind, but it had died down since that morning. I picked up the steady hum of traffic on the highway and the piercing cries of birds heading to roost, but from the sixth floor of the high-rise, the day-to-day noises were less abrasive, allowing me a greater sense of solitude.

I ran my hands along the curve of my bow to calm my nerves and then set up my tripod. With my foot in the locater at the base, I raised the bow until the back of my left hand hit the rubber ball on top of the tripod, marking my elevation. Slowly, I drew my fingers back toward my cheek, then let go to release an arc of air. When I drew again, I focused on the angle of my elbow and the gentle pressure of wind nudging my aim to the right.

The practice soothed me, but just as my thoughts began to settle, a scream shook my bones. Loud, panicked — a sound of agony. This high up, I knew the source couldn't be far. Right across from me, if I had to guess.

With my heart in my throat, I tripped over my cane and jumped for the balcony door, planning to get my parents so we could call the police. But the screams got louder, more urgent, and without thinking, I tightened my fingers around my bow and turned around. My foot caught on the foot guide and the tripod toppled over, but before I could bend down to grab it, the cries morphed into a stomach-churning wail, and I knew my time was short. Mentally crossing my fingers that my ears would be enough to guide my aim in the right direction, I grabbed an arrow and raised the bow with trembling hands. I focused on my breathing and lost myself to my training. Breath, draw, breath...release.

Across the alley, glass shattered, and by the way the screams grew louder, I knew I'd found the right place. I was amazed that no sirens had come blaring up the street from the noise, but I couldn't wait for them to arrive — the man sounded as though he were being torn in half. His voice had dropped to a lower tenor, a raspy, grating noise that burrowed deep in my ears and vibrated against my brain.

Following the sound, I aimed again and sent up a silent prayer that the wind would stay with me. I wanted to startle, not kill. With a deep breath, I steadied my stance, emptied my mind, and loosed the second arrow.

The screams stopped so abruptly that my heart jumped into my throat with the thought that I'd hit someone, but a moment later I heard shouts and the distinct sounds of a fight. Something was smashed — big, like furniture — and then heavy footsteps clanged down the fire escape.

Again, I debated telling my parents so we could call the police, but now two of my arrows would be in the person's apartment, and I didn't think anyone would look too kindly on that.

I don't know where my decision came from,

whether it was bravery or stupidity that compelled me, but I slid my bow over my shoulder, picked my cane up off the balcony floor, and stepped into the apartment.

I expected the adults to ask me what had happened — to my ears, the sound of the fight across the alley had been loud enough to drown out the soft music playing on the stereo — and yet when I entered the living room, I interrupted a mix of relaxed laughter and groans, no doubt from one of my father's horrible jokes.

"Molly, honey, are you all right?" my mother asked. I heard her rise off the couch and approach me. "You're white as a ghost." Her soft fingers brushed my cheek and she pressed the back of her hand on my forehead. "No fever, but you're sweating. Is everything okay?"

I forced a smile, half of my brain wondering how I had heard something no one else seemed to, and the other half working on plausible excuses to run out of the apartment and get across the street. "I'm fine. It's just been a long day. I might take a bit of a walk to clear my head. Walk off those delicious mashed potatoes."

I tried to appeal to my father with the horrible jokes and my mother with the compliment, but still I picked up the hesitation and uncertainty in Dad's voice when he said, "With your bow?"

I widened my smile. "It's a talking piece. You're always telling me to be more social. I'll be back in a few minutes."

"All right, dear," said Mom before Dad pushed any further. I didn't think I'd be able to fake my way through many more lies, so I was glad she let things go, as she usually did. I sensed Dad's objection, the way he cleared his throat and mumbled something under his breath, but he didn't argue.

I took the elevator to street level and stepped out into the chilly evening air. A few droplets of rain fell on my forehead, but the weather held off until I reached the lobby of the building across the alley.

Someone else was getting on the elevator, so I followed them on.

"Floor?" he asked.

I rushed through the logic of where I was going, a very loud voice in my head telling me to be smart and go home, but I'd been on the sixth floor and swore the apartment had been close, so I said the sixth.

"Only goes up to five."

I cleared my throat. "Five, then. Please."

He got out somewhere along the way, and I took

the rest of the trip up to the top floor, striking east after I got out. I tapped my cane against the baseboard and listened for the sound to change when I reached the door. I hitched my bow up on my shoulder and turned my right ear toward the apartment, straining to pick up any noises from inside.

Someone walking around, a groan, glass being swept up or kicked aside.

Exhaling slowly, I knocked.

A few moments later, the door opened. Although the man — or so I guessed by the smell of spiced body wash — said nothing, I sensed his surprise to find me on his doorstep.

"Can I help you?" He asked, confirming my guess. His voice was rough and hoarse, as though he'd exerted himself. Which, I supposed, made sense. I couldn't tell yet from the few words he'd spoken if he'd been the one screaming.

"I was over across the way and thought I heard a fight. Wanted to make sure everyone was okay."

"And you took the risk of coming alone?" No parental worry, only surprise with a hint of amusement.

"No one can accuse me of sitting on my ass, at least," I replied. "Are you all right?"

"Fine, kid. Just fine. Had a misunderstanding

with a work colleague. You know how these things go."

I didn't, so I stayed quiet. I wondered how I was going to retrieve my arrows before my parents noticed two were missing.

The guy made it easy.

"Wild stab in the dark that you were the person who saved my life?"

A slight stumble in his tone. He'd aimed for grateful, but halfway through the sentence I picked up the smallest trace of annoyance.

"That was me," I said. "Sorry about your window."

"Oh, god, don't even worry about that. Fixing the thing wouldn't have mattered if I were dead. Come on in a minute and I'll get your arrows. I'm Jermaine, by the way."

"Molly," I replied, and cocked my head to follow his footsteps, not taking more than two steps into the apartment. I made sure to keep my foot propped against the door so it wouldn't swing shut behind me.

"You have pretty incredible skills, Molly," he said from across the room. "You practice a lot?"

"A few hours a day."

"That's dedication." He was impressed, and I got the sense he was walking around an idea, using his questions to put feelers out.

Glass crunched under his shoes, and when he spoke again, he stood facing me.

"The other arrow doesn't seem to be here. He must have taken it when he ran."

I cursed under my breath, wondering how I would explain that to my parents.

Before I had too much time to mull, he shocked me by saying, "I don't suppose you'd be interested in earning some cash doing a few odd jobs for me? You're obviously capable, and I'm sure your competitions don't run cheap. I could use someone like you for my business."

I kept my expression neutral as best I could. "What's your business?"

He chuckled. "Don't think that today was any indication of my regular habits. I'm a scientist first and foremost. Research into the nature of our being. Fascinating work, but harmless, I promise."

His shoes crunched over broken glass, moving toward me, and I tensed. He paused a few feet away, but I didn't relax my grip around my cane.

"Your arrow," he said.

I extended my hand, and he dropped it across my palm, its weight familiar and reassuring.

"So, what do you say?"

I frowned. "Thanks for the offer, but I don't

think I can take you up on it. Between school and practice I'd never have the time, and I doubt my parents would approve."

Plus I believe you're a great, lying sack of shit, and I wouldn't trust you as far as I could shoot.

"That's unfortunate," he said, and the change in his tone sent a shooting fear down my spine. My grip around my arrow and cane grew clammy, and my heart shifted up into my throat.

He closed the distance between us and wrapped his fingers around my arm, squeezing tightly.

"I do wish you'd reconsider. You cost me a pretty penny today in equipment, and lost me a specimen so rare I doubt I'll ever find one again. I'd say you owed me a few favors, don't you?"

My arm throbbed under the increasing pressure of his squeeze, but I refused to react. Years of getting bullied in school had taught me how to deal with people like him, and my parents had always encouraged extra education. I twisted my arm to bend his wrist and jerked away once his hold loosened. In a fluid, practiced motion, I dropped my shoulder so my bow slid down my arm to my hand and nocked the arrow he'd handed me. My cane clattered to the floor.

"Considering what I interrupted in this room, I don't feel I owe you anything," I said. "Just be grateful I didn't call the cops."

I took a step backward, accepting that my cane would be left behind.

"Now, if you don't want me lodging a third arrow somewhere in you, I would very much appreciate you taking three steps back. And do not," I rushed to add when I sensed him coming closer, "think for a minute that I will hesitate."

Jermaine sniffed, but the air around me cleared when he moved away. Although I was curious about why he would just let me go, I was too relieved to question it.

"Pleasure to meet you, Jermaine," I said, one foot in the hallway. "Please don't be offended if I say I hope to never hear your voice again."

Not waiting for him to reply, I turned and ran for the elevator with one hand outstretched to guide my way. I didn't breathe until I'd fumbled the cage door closed and hit the button for the lobby.

"I don't believe your story on so many levels. Hell, I wouldn't even buy it as a fictional tale," Daphne said. "Why would a bright girl be so stupid as to go to a strange man's house because she heard a fight? And I don't care how good an archer you claim to be, you're no superhero. Those would have been two impossible shots. Plus Jermaine wouldn't have just let you go after you turned him down. You've heard all about him by now. He would have fried your ass."

"It does sound rather implausible," Allegra agreed.

"I like the story," said Gabe, slapping the table. "Gives me hope that the human race isn't as doomed as I fear it is. But I will concede it's a difficult tale to swallow."

Antony picked a spot of lint off his knee. "It sounds like the little girl wants to keep up with the grown-up players."

Vera's gray gaze roved over each of them, sliding to Zachariel when the daemelus brought his fist down on the table.

Beside him, Molly jumped and raised her cane as though prepared to use it to fight him off.

"Do not accuse her of lying," he growled, his brown eyes swirling with a reddish hue. "I can attest to her story. I watched from below, saw that monster move into the window to search for her arrow. I couldn't pick up any of the conversation, but I saw Molly run back to the other apartment building, and a moment later, Jermaine appeared in the window again. She is not guilty of this crime."

Gabe grinned. "How about that? For the first time up we have witnesses. I guess we can rule you two out, big guy."

The red in Zachariel's eyes faded, but returned in a flare when Allegra quirked a smooth eyebrow and said, "Not necessarily."

"Explain," he grumbled.

"You seem terribly protective of this human. I would not be surprised if it turned out you are lying to protect her."

Molly twisted in her seat toward him, surprise etched on her face. Glowering, Zachariel reached into the deep pockets of his coat, drew out the arrow he'd taken from the shattered glass, and slammed it on the table.

"This girl saved my life," he said. "For that I am in her debt until the opportunity arises to return the favor. If I were lying, I would consider the favor repaid."

Molly's brow furrowed. "You're not paranoid if someone is actually following you. I knew there was someone." She paused. "Not sure how I feel about that, actually."

She slid her hand over the table and ran her fingers over the arrow point before drawing it closer to her.

Zachariel said nothing, just turned to Vera as though awaiting her judgment. She stared back at him, considering, her long fingers tapping against her arm.

"We'll pay these two the same courtesy as we have everyone else so far and defer any accusations until we have time to evaluate the stories." A red eyebrow rose on her pale forehead. "Because unless someone would like to change his mind and confess, it's clear not everyone has told the entire truth."

A deep hush fell on the table as the enormity of the moment sank in.

Each person had shared his or her story, and at face value, each had come across as genuine. The confusion, the disdain, the discomfort written on the storytellers' faces had seemed sincere.

But Jermaine had been so certain that one of them had done it.

They remained in silence until Molly's stomach

grumbled, a reminder that time was passing and they wouldn't be able to leave until they'd reached some sort of conclusion.

"What happens if he got it wrong?" Daphne asked. "What if it was someone else? The guy was an asshole — he probably pissed off more than the seven of us."

"That's irrelevant," Allegra snapped. "He believed it to be one of us, so one of us must play the sacrifice."

"I vote for the human child," said Antony. "She's the easiest one to kill."

Zachariel's chair flipped backward as he leaped to his feet. "I wish you would try. It would clear my debt to her all too quickly if I had the pleasure of tearing your head from your shoulders."

Molly shifted warily away from Antony, but he remained still and smiling. Gabe broke the tension with a laugh.

"Angelic nobility with a demonic temper. Zach, you are an absolutely fascinating creature."

Zachariel growled again and Vera raised a hand. "Let us calm down. Zachariel, please sit. I promise no one will raise a hand against Molly unless we prove beyond a doubt that she is the culprit."

The daemelus hesitated before complying. Molly's expression turned more fearful at the insinuation that her story might not have been believed.

"I swear I told you the truth. I had no reason to kill him. I had no idea who he was, let alone that he was an evil son of a whats-its. I swear I'm not lying."

Vera dropped her chin in a nod. "Be that as it may, someone around this table is."

Six voices broke out in protest with varying volumes of resentment and hurt. Each person fought for the floor, so no one could be understood. Denials and insults were buried under the din.

Vera finally raised a hand again to quiet them and gestured to Molly. "You were trying to say?"

The girl cleared her throat and shifted in her chair. "I said if you were looking for liars, you were right."

A few new mumbles rose up, but Vera quelled them with her sharp gray stare.

"Go on," she said.

"I might not be able to see your faces or use crazy superpowers like some of you people, but I've had to develop my own skills. Since I can't read body language, I've trained myself to pick up vocal cues, and I can say without a doubt that at least three people here lied."

Daphne barked a laugh. "That's rich. Nice cover up there, kid, but you can't deflect suspicion away that easily."

"Neither can you," said Molly, "since you were one of the liars."

The sorceress's jaw dropped and her eyes widened. She sputtered, offended.

"And the other two?" Vera asked before she could say anything.

"Gabriel," Molly said. "And Antony. It's possible others did, too, but those are the lies I heard."

"This is preposterous!" Daphne exclaimed. "Are you really going to take the word of a kid who not only knows nothing about our world, but can barely make her way through her own?"

Molly's eyebrows rose, but before she could retort, Gabe laughed again. "The lady doth protest too much, methinks."

"Well, are you going to stand for it?" Daphne demanded. "You're accused of lying, too."

"I am. And I did. I won't try to deny it in the face of someone who knows what she's talking about."

His admission left Daphne staggered, but she only needed a moment to find her footing.

"Well, I'm not lying," she said to Vera. "Make him tell you the truth if he admits to it. Save us all a lot of time."

Vera looked to Gabe, her expression exuding patience.

He shrugged. "I don't mind telling you. But I know my lie, so that's boring. I'm more interested in hers."

"I'm not lying!" Daphne shouted.

Allegra winced. "Shrieking will not convince us, my dear. At this point no one believes you, so you might as well come out with it."

Daphne's green eyes grew round with panic, and she picked at her fingernails as she scanned the room, searching for a friendly face. When she found none, her shoulders slumped, and the haughty expression she'd worn since her arrival faded. Without it, she looked small — like someone trying hard to be somebody and never quite making it.

"Fine, I lied. But I didn't kill him." At the quiet anticipation around the table, she puffed out a breath and shoved her fingers through her hair. "I knew what Jermaine had planned, all right? I knew he intended to use human sacrifices for his spell, and I still agreed to help him."

Tears filled her eyes, but she didn't let them fall.

"I've worked so hard for so long with nothing to show for it, so when Jermaine approached me with his idea...how could I turn away?"

She looked pleadingly to Vera, and then to Allegra, then Gabe — las though they might reassure her they would have made the same decision.

When no one said anything, she wiped her eyes on the edge of her sleeve and raised a shoulder.

"But at the last minute, I couldn't go through with it. They looked so scared and helpless, and I imagined the pain they'd feel once the ritual started. I couldn't do it." She snorted. "Turns out I have more empathy than ambition. Just my luck, huh? Anyway, the rest of the story is true enough. We fought, he got away, and I ended up with a bit more power than I had when I went in. So I guess I did win in the end. In a way."

She fell silent and focused on her nails, her left thumbnail nearly torn to the quick.

"Molly?" Vera asked.

The girl tilted her head, considering, and then nodded. "I'm not a human polygraph or anything, but it sounded like she told the truth that time."

Daphne sniffled, and Allegra handed her a handkerchief from her handbag, cringing slightly when the other woman blew her nose into it.

Vera shifted toward Gabe. "Your turn."

"Anything you command," he replied with a

bow of his head and a sweep of his hand. "Like I said, I have nothing to hide — I just didn't want to raise suspicions against me if I didn't have to. I confess, I didn't leave Jermaine's place quite as quickly or quietly as I claimed. I tried to kill the son of a bitch."

A few gasps rose up from the table, but not everyone appeared surprised. Vera's stoicism remained intact, and Antony's smile turned smug.

"Of course I would," Gabe continued. "It would have been stupid not to. That guy had come after me more than once, and I doubted he had any intention of giving up. My attack was perfectly justified."

"How can we believe this version of your story?" Allegra asked. "As you said earlier, if you had wanted him dead, you could have turned him to stone. So I think you are leaving out one or two important details."

"Sure," Gabe agreed. "Could have turned him to stone and had everyone know it was me. Give me a little more credit than that."

"So you attempted hand-to-hand combat and lost?" Zachariel asked.

Gabe slapped his hand on his chest as though his ego had been wounded. "Alas, it's true. My fisticuff skills were not enough to outmatch his. So

I bolted before I had the indignity of losing to a cow patty like him. And there's my crazy lie. Hardly worth the retelling, am I right? What do you say, kid? Did I nail it this time?"

Molly's smile gave away not only that she believed him, but also how far his roguish charm had won her over. She nodded. "Again, you could just be covering your lies better this time, but I'd buy it."

Another hush fell over the table as everyone's attention returned to Antony. A crease of annoyance appeared on his brow.

"You all turn to me as though you've already made up your minds. I can't say I appreciate that you're all so keen to blame me."

"Then prove us wrong, brother," said Allegra. "If we have to extend this interrogation to a second round of stories and evidence, then tell us the truth so we can move on."

"It has to be him, right?" said Daphne. "He's the only other one who lied."

"The girl has said she is not infallible," Allegra argued.

"I don't need you to defend me." Antony's words came out in such a soft, venomous hiss that everyone's attention jumped back to him. "You of all people."

"What?" His sister's gold-brown eyes flew wide, filled with confusion.

"You had to have him for yourself, didn't you? A whole world of men falling at your feet, and you chose him."

Allegra's confusion morphed into incredulity. "Antony, you cannot be serious. Obviously, I had no idea you were interested in Jermaine."

"You taint everything, you foul witch," he spat. "You always have."

She laughed. "Antony, really."

But her laugh fizzled out and her amusement faded at the sight of her brother's eyes glowing gold with fury.

"Tell us what happened, Antony," said Vera.

Antony growled, refusing to tear his gaze away from Allegra, and said, "We were going to take over the underworld. We had it all planned out, and then you —"

"Start at the beginning," Vera interjected, and this time her soft voice drew his attention.

The glow faded from his eyes and he collected himself, smoothing his pant leg and crossing his hands on the table as though his restraint had never slipped.

"My story was entirely truthful," he said. "I just chose to end it at the most important part.

Jermaine and I met years ago, and I believe I knew him better than any of you. Not that there was much sentiment between us, but we were both strong. Ambitious." The corners of his lips curled upward. "You all believe he was the sole mastermind, but I was there for all of it. Behind the scenes. Moving the game pieces so Jermaine might have more room for success. You six might have gotten away temporarily, but you have no idea how far our reach was. A few more months, a few more rituals, and we would have had all of you eating out of our hands."

He curled his hands into fists and returned his focus to Allegra. "Then you had to show up. My dear, sweet, spoiled sister." Each word was spoken with slow, enunciated rage. "What we had was a perfect partnership, until the day he told me about you. Had no idea you were my sister, of course. Just thought I'd be interested in what you were and what you tried to do. I admit, I didn't handle it as well as I might have. I accused him of being careless, of risking everything we'd worked for. I threw all of his old mistakes in his face, and the more I accused him of, the more he confessed. Murders I hadn't known about, other plans he had in the works behind my back. He'd betrayed me."

He dropped his gaze to his fists and

straightened his fingers, the joints popping with tension. "I hit him. He fought back. I couldn't even tell you how it happened. His window was broken, we got too close, and he fell. That was that."

Belying his attempt to appear calm, his fingers wound back toward his palm, and when he raised his head again, the golden glow in his eyes had returned. Zachariel and Gabe raised their hands in reaction to the burn of Antony's anger.

"And none of it would have happened if not for you," he hissed at Allegra. "I had a plan. We could have succeeded in everything. If not for you!"

He lunged across the table toward his sister, his fingers out like claws, his lip pulled back in a snarl. Allegra jumped to her feet, her chair clattering to the floor, and Daphne stood beside her to grab her arm and pull her away. Zachariel grabbed his ankle and jerked him back.

Molly rose to her feet and ran her hand over the table as though to ground herself. Her head twitched to follow the sounds of the fight, her eyebrows raised in alarm.

Antony kicked out his free leg, catching Gabe in the jaw and jarring off his sunglasses.

The Gorgon swung his head away, his eyes squeezed shut, while Zachariel pushed Molly clear of Antony's flailing legs. She backed away until her hands hit the wall and then dropped into a crouch, her face pinched with fear and uncertainty.

Antony flipped onto his back and sat up, hands clawing at Zachariel's eyes until blood streamed down the daemelus's face from the scratches. His foot caught Gabe's cheek as he bent to retrieve his sunglasses.

"Dammit, Gabe, just look him in the eye!" Daphne cried. She raised her hands, but no magic came. She lunged at Antony to pull his attention away from Zachariel, and he swung his fist at her. She fell over Allegra's chair, blood sliding over her cheek where his ring had cut through the skin.

Antony hooked his fingers around the opposite end of the table to continue his attack on Daphne, and Zachariel's grip on his legs slipped. He lost his balance, tripped over his chair, and the leg snapped under his weight as he fell to the floor.

Vera finally stood up. Her face blank of expression, she closed her fingers around Antony's throat before he had an opportunity to launch himself in Allegra's direction. His sister stood frozen in shock. Her hand rested on her chest, her breath quick and shallow.

"That is more than enough," Vera said.

The glow in Antony's eyes flared, enough heat simmering off his skin to create a haze around him.

He inhaled slowly and Vera flinched, pressing her lips together. She squeezed his throat harder, ignoring the burns and blisters marring her wrist where he wrapped his hands around it to pull her away.

His clothes began to smoke. Tears streamed down Vera's face, her knuckles white as she increased the pressure. But it had no effect. He struck his fists against the table and left charred stains behind.

Zachariel threw his weight over Antony's legs, his own skin turning red and scaled at the heat.

His strength clearly growing in his anger, Antony wrenched himself free of Vera, jerked one of his feet free and slammed the sole of his leather shoe into Zachariel's nose. Then he threw himself off the table toward Molly. They rolled onto the floor and he wrapped his hand around her chin, trying to force her face toward him to press his mouth over hers. She flailed against him, but he was too strong, and with every deep inhale Antony took, she screamed in agony.

The daemelus let out a chest-deep growl and his red-scaled hands reached for Antony's waist. But before he had a chance to fulfill his debt, an arrow plunged through the incubus's jugular, the sharp spike tearing through his throat and out the back of his neck. Antony's eyes flew wide, his lips parted with a breathless exclamation, and then he rolled over onto his back.

Allegra released a cry. She rushed to his side and knelt down, the hem of her green dress dipping into the blood pooling under Antony's head. His hand twitched toward her, but she didn't take it. A series of expressions crossed her delicate features, but surprise won when her brother used his last amount of energy to jab his hand toward her throat, his own face twisted with loathing. She jumped to her feet to dodge the strike, and he gurgled his despair. His arm went slack, and his skin wrinkled as his heat evaporated. The glow in his eyes faded to nothing.

In stunned silence, the others stared at the fingers gripping the arrow, their gazes traveling up the arm toward Molly's face, her fair skin ashen, her lip wobbling with panic. Blood spattered her arms and stained her shirt. There were burns on her neck and around her face where Antony had grabbed her.

A sudden flash of light blinded everyone in the room, and by the time it faded, five people stood in a brightly lit, spacious apartment, with a sixth person on the floor. A white leather couch sat on one side of the room, a broken desk in the opposite corner. A smashed domed window overlooked the fire escape.

Vera bent to help up a trembling Molly and draped her arm around the girl's shoulders. Zachariel shifted closer, moving between them and Allegra, as though anticipating the sister to avenge her brother. But Allegra stood staring where Antony had lain a moment ago, her expression full of sadness. Daphne stepped toward her with a box of tissues she'd grabbed from the end table. She offered it to Allegra, but the succubus shook her head.

"There were twenty-five of us in the family," she said, her voice hollow. "Of all my brothers and sisters, he was the only one I never tried to kill. In all those years, I never knew how much he hated me."

"I don't know if I would take it so personally," said Gabe. He leaned back against the dining table and adjusted his sunglasses, making sure the bent frames kept his gaze guarded. "Jermaine had a way of messing people up inside."

"I think Antony cared about him a lot," said Molly, and although her voice sounded calm, tears spilled over onto her cheeks. "That's why the betrayal hurt him so badly. At least, that's what it sounded like to me."

A silence stretched out until Daphne released a breath. "Well, it's over now, at least."

"So what's next?" asked Gabe.

"Is there a next?" Allegra asked. "We fulfilled what Jermaine intended for us to do. We solved the mystery. Now we return to our lives."

"Can we?" he asked. "I don't know about the rest of you, but I don't feel I'm the same person I was when I went into that room. Never knew there were so many other freaks like me in this city for one thing."

"So what do you suggest?" Daphne asked. "That we exchange email addresses and keep up correspondence?"

"Don't you feel we should do *something*?"

He looked around and shrugged when no one replied.

"The only thing I would like to do is go home," said Allegra, and she started toward the door. "Soak in a long hot bath. Drink a bottle of champagne."

"That sounds perfect," Daphne sighed, and followed her. "Throw on my PJs and eat a full box of chocolate caramels."

Allegra nodded. "And then go out to a bar and find a man to bring home."

Daphne cleared her throat and reached for the door handle. "I'll leave that part to you. I think I'm off men for a while."

Allegra winked. "There are other options."

Daphne's eyes widened and they both disappeared around the corner.

"I should probably get home, too," said Molly. "I have no idea how long I've been gone. My parents are probably freaking out. And now I'm going to have to come up with a good story for the burns. I'll say I tripped over a steam grate or something." She hesitated and then added, "Is it weird for me to say thank you? It's been a surreal and terrifying day, and I might wake up tomorrow believing everything was a dream, but it'll be a dream I remember for the rest of my life. I don't think I would have survived it if not for you guys. Antony really did want to kill me."

"It's us who should be thanking you," Vera replied, resting her hand on Molly's shoulder. "You helped us narrow the stories down to him, and if he'd gotten free in the end, I believe he would have tried to kill us all. Demons are powerful and unpredictable. Rarely to be trusted. No offense intended, Zachariel. I appreciate your help."

"None taken," he replied in his gruff voice. He glanced at his arm in time to see the red scales fade once more into the appearance of human flesh.

"Take care of yourself, kid," said Gabe.

Zachariel took another step toward her. "I can see you home, Molly. Make sure you get there safely."

She raised an eyebrow. "Did you mean what you said before? Are you really going to follow me around until you have a chance to save my life?"

"Yes."

"You know you don't have to do that. I don't feel like you owe me anything. I just wanted to help."

"Honor requires the debt be paid. Also, I admire your bravery, which is impressive for a human. It will interest me to see how well you do."

He spoke with straight-faced sincerity, but Molly smiled. "Well, all right. I suppose life could be interesting with a — what did he call you? A daemelus following me around. Maybe it'll help convince me that all this really happened. That this whole other world really exists."

"And you, Zachariel?" Vera asked. "You sought Jermaine out for a reason. Will you continue your search for a side?"

The angel-demon stared at Molly, and then at the broken window. "Perhaps it's time I created my own side. Jermaine was a cruel man, but he was right about one thing — both halves of my nature give me strength. Perhaps it would be unwise to close myself off from either of them."

He nodded to Vera and Gabe, then followed Molly out of the apartment.

"So that was a day," said Gabe.

"It was indeed," Vera replied, tearing her attention away from the doorway. "Certainly not what my schedule looked like when I woke up in the morning."

Gabe smiled. The crinkling of his cheeks shook his glasses loose, and they tumbled to the floor. For the briefest moment, his golden eyes met her gray ones. He jerked his head away and slammed his fist down on the dining table.

Vera stood frozen.

Then she bent down and retrieved his glasses. Using the strength of her long fingers, she bent the frames into their proper shape and set them down on the table top.

At the sound of the glasses hitting the wood, Gabe slowly opened his eyes, the irises swirls of green and gold. He looked up into Vera's calm gaze and then scanned the way she stood with her arms crossed and her hip propped against the table.

"This is new," he said. His tone aimed for nonchalant, but the tremor betrayed his awe.

"I enjoy taking people by surprise," she replied with the faintest hint of a smile.

"You've certainly done that more than once

today." He paused, and his charming smile appeared. "I don't suppose you want to go grab a drink?"

Vera's eyes crinkled in the corners. "I need to get home to my dogs. Goodbye, Gabriel. It was nice to meet you."

Her hair swayed as she made her way to the door, and Gabe's gaze remained glued to her hips. For a moment, just when she reached the doorway, she glanced back. Then she was gone.

Chuckling, he reached for his glasses and settled them on his nose. The movement caused something to crinkle in his pocket, and he dipped his hand into his trench coat to pull out a sheet of paper.

Jermaine's letter.

Scanning it over again, he lingered on the last paragraph. *The semi-goddess, the Gorgon-fae, the incubus, the succubus, the daemelus, the sorceress, and the human — such a unique collection for this invisible entente.*

Gabe laughed and shook his head. "The Invisible Entente. I like that." He patted the table. "Well, Jermaine, it's been fun. Rest in hell, buddy."

He drew a line in the air and a doorway opened before him, another apartment — this one much messier and warmer — appearing beyond. He stepped through and the doorway closed, leaving nothing behind but emptiness.

THANK YOU FOR READING

If you enjoyed the read, please help support the author by leaving a review at the retailer where you purchased the book. Reviews make a world of difference for an author, helping us reach new audiences and bringing more people into the worlds you've spent time in

For exclusive character content, announcements, promotions, and special offers, sign up for Krista's mailing list at http://eepurl.com/GIJkz

ACKNOWLEDGMENTS

It's always scary moving on to a new project when people are used to a certain world with certain characters, so I owe a huge thank-you to the people who helped make the transition not only easy, but fun.

Thanks to my editor, Sue Archer, for being an integral part of bringing these characters to life, fleshing them out, and making them step off the page with such detail, and to my cover artist, Ravven, for taking this fictional world out of my head and giving it such beauty and colour. More thanks to my readers — Colin, Dean, Deb, Keith, and Brenda — for helping me work out the story and smooth out the rough edges. And the deepest gratitude to Chris Reddie, who read for me, created the logo for the series, and held my hand from first draft to final.

I created this story as a thank-you to my readers, but the more I wrote, the more I realized there could be more in store for this mishmash of supernatural creatures. I hope you enjoy the story and are ready for more from the Invisible Entente.

OTHER WORKS BY KRISTA WALSH
www.kristawalshauthor.com

The Meratis Trilogy

Evensong
Eventide
Evenlight

The Cadis Trilogy

Bloodlore
Blightlore
Bladelore

ABOUT THE AUTHOR

Known for witty, vivid characters, Krista Walsh never has more fun than getting them into trouble and taking her time getting them out. When not writing, she can be found walking, reading, gaming, or watching a film – anything to get lost in a good story.
She currently lives in Ottawa, Ontario.

You can connect via her website:
www.kristawalshauthor.com

88146452R00088

Made in the USA
Columbia, SC
01 February 2018